MW01199951

The Cowboy and His Secret

Rock Springs Texas Book 5

Kaci M. Rose

Five Little Roses Publishing

Book Cover By: **Sarah Kil Creative Studio**

Editing By: Anna @ Indie Hub

Blurb

"I'll do whatever it takes to make her mine."
Sarah

I have a secret. I've been in love with a cowboy since I was sixteen. For years I wouldn't admit it to myself, because I was focused on becoming a teacher. But after graduating and being forced to take a job as a waitress, I find myself in a situation where only Mac can help. A dark threat is closing in and he is my only hope of escape.

Mac

I still remember the first time I saw Sarah. We were both teenagers, and she was swimming in the lake wearing a sexy red bikini. Since then, I've ached for her. But she had big dreams, so I settled for friendship. Until she finished college... Now, I plan to do whatever it takes to make her mine. Step one will mean helping her ditch her skeevy boss.

Step two? Find out who is stalking her and why.

Come meet the small town of Rock Springs, Texas, with a family that has your back, a town that knows your business, and men who love with everything they have.

Warning

This is a cowboy romance with a sexy cowboy and a strong woman who have a lot of heat! This sexy full-length romance. Complete with a happy ever after, no cheating, and no cliffhanger!

This book may have some trigger points centering around abuse and what makes these characters strong and protective and justice is always served!

Readers 18+, please.

Dedication

To the coffee that kept me going and the kids that call me Mommy.

Contents

Get Free Books!

Prologue

Mac

7 Years Ago

My adoption is official, and I am now part of the only family I have ever known. Mom and Dad are amazing, and my new siblings are my best friends. I may be the youngest at just sixteen, but I have been living here for well over a year now.

It's spring break, and the ranch just finished all their spring checks in what we love to call hell week. This is my first trip up to the family lake house and I'm excited, it is also my first vacation of any kind. I grew up on the local Native American reservation and while my father would travel for business, he never took me. So other than heading to Dallas I've never really been anywhere, can't say I mind though.

The trip to Walker Lake consisted of miles of North Texas landscape, bluebells, and longhorn cattle made up the bulk of it. Walker Lake is an hour outside Amarillo, so Mom and Dad promise to take us kids up that way to see part of Route 66 this trip.

The drive goes by a lot faster than I expect and before I know it, we pull into a beautiful home that looks almost like a large log cabin. It's bigger than I had imagined, but then this family doesn't do anything small with six of us kids now.

"Beautiful isn't it?" Sage walks up beside me. "It's so relaxing, you will come out of here ready to tackle the rest of the school year."

She loops her arms through mine as we head inside. Sage is the whole reason I'm here. She recognized that my father was abusive because she had been through it with her biological parents. She inserted herself into my life at a time that I just wanted to hide.

She gave me these guys as friends and now family. She is also the one who saved my life and stopped my dad from almost killing me. I shake the dark thoughts from my head, this trip is about relaxing and regrouping, not taking a walk down memory lane.

"Here, Mac, let me show you to your room. Each of you kids will have your own and then there is a huge walkout basement perfect for grandkids to bunk in later on," Mom says and winks at me.

"Mom, we just got him in the family, don't send him running for the hills with talks of grandbabies already," Sage jokes. I just offer up a half-smile. Mom is already hungry for grandbabies, with Jason being an adult and Colt, Sage, and Blaze graduating high school in just a few months.

Later that day, after we all get settled, we head down to the lake to swim. We plan to have dinner down there too but before that Jason, Blaze, and Colt help blow up one of those water slides that floats in the water like a raft. I've never seen anything like it as I watch them flying down it, doing all sorts of tricks.

I hear laughter to my right a few houses down, and as I look over the most beautiful girl I have ever seen steps out of the water. Her golden hair is still dry as it hangs down just past her shoulder like she just stepped in to cool off for a moment. She is laughing with another girl, and as she reaches for her towel, her eyes lock with mine.

Then she waves, and something sparks in my chest. Sage once told me that she knew I would be in her family because she got the feeling. I asked her about it, and she said it's a feeling you get when you know someone is meant to be in your life for the long haul. When you know they are important and that you would be a complete idiot to walk away.

That's the feeling that hits me.

"Hey, I'll be right back," I call over my shoulder and start walking toward this girl.

She waves when she sees me coming toward her and her smile stays on her face. That smile is one I know I will need to make sure is on there often.

"Hey, I'm Makya, but everyone calls me Mac, I'm here for the week with my family." I point over my shoulder.

"I'm Sarah and this is my friend Sky." Sky has a very boho look to her with long brown hair but it's Sarah who draws my attention with her dark blond hair which frames her face, and rich brown eyes that I struggle to tear my gaze from.

"That your family's lake house?" Sky asks.

"Yeah. This yours?" I ask Sarah

"No, it's Sky's parents. They live here all year. I've met Megan and Sage before, but I haven't seen you around."

I nod. "It's my first time here. Mom and Dad adopted me officially a few months back. We're getting ready to eat, and Mom cooks enough for an army, why don't you two join us?"

They look at each other and Sky shrugs and Sarah looks back at me. "Okay, I don't have to be home until later."

"You live in town too?" I ask as we walk back toward my family.

"Yeah, on the other side of town." She points. "But I'm over here all the time with Sky."

I shove my hands into my pockets because it takes everything not to reach out and touch her.

"Mom, Dad, this is Sky and Sarah. I invited them to eat with us."

"Oh, that's wonderful we need more girls here. Sky? It's your parents who own the house over there, right?" my mom asks as she hugs them both.

"Yes ma'am," Sky answers.

"Oh, none of that ma'am stuff here. I'm Helen and you girls are welcome anytime."

We spent the whole rest of the week like that. The girls coming over and spending the day with us and the more time I spent with Sarah, the more time I wanted with her and the more I knew she would be in my life for good.

Chapter 1

Mac

I love my time at the lake house. Ever since that first time here when I met Sarah, we spend every possible minute together when I visit. I had such a crush on her right from the start, and it grows every time I see her.

When she headed off to college, we started texting and emailing more and more, phone calls came later. Being able to talk to her makes the distance a bit easier.

I was so excited for her to get her degree that had been her dream for so long. The feelings I had for her quickly grew but I didn't admit to myself until I saw Blaze and Riley together that what I felt was love. Though at twenty-three, I didn't think I'd find love so soon.

I guess I always knew because no one compared to her. I tried a few dates but always cut them off early, and the tribe has tried to set me up with a few girls, but they just can't hold a candle to the way I feel about Sarah.

Over the last year, we've started doing more video calls, and since she's graduated it's become every night.

I know she's in town, so this trip with the family couldn't have been planned any better. Jason and Ella just got married and they spent a week here before they asked us all to join them. Blaze and Riley did the same thing for their honeymoon, wanting to give the girls the full lake house, family experience.

Sage and Colt are married now, they had been dancing around each other for as long as I had known them. And Megan finally admitted that Hunter was more than a friend and they are married too. I'm the last single guy because my girl has big dreams and I plan to help her reach every one of them. Settling down in the small ranching town of Rock Springs, Texas, isn't on her list right now.

I love the ranch and the land, plus the tribe is here and I don't think I could ever leave them behind. I don't know where that leaves Sarah and me, but I know I can't walk away from her either.

I hate feeling like I have to give one up to have the other and those thoughts have been cycling through my head for the last year.

I walk around the lake house taking it all in. Mom's made a few small changes since we were here last, but nothing major.

The living room, kitchen, and dining room all have a view out the back of the house overlooking the lake. Toward the front of the house are all the kid's bedrooms. We each have our own. Downstairs is a game room, movie theater, dry bar, and a huge open space perfect for putting grandbabies, as Mom says. Now that grandbabies are on the way, Mom is starting to redesign this space.

I have always found this place calming and a great place to think. The wood walls and stone accents give the place a back to nature feel that blends well with the lake. I guess this is why Mom and Dad fell in love with the house too. Their bedroom is on the far side next to the kitchen, and it's a show-stopper designed around the lake view. There is no way you couldn't start your day off being relaxed waking up to that view. Well, unless it was catching Blaze jumping in the lake butt naked on a dare, which happened a few years back. I haven't heard Mom and Dad yelling like that in a while, because unless you are Riley, really no one wants to see that, much less as the first thing they see when they open their eyes.

I head out to the deck where everyone is and sit down to just watch my family. Ella just told Megan she wants to go to cosmetology school and work in Megan's beauty shop when she graduates. It's great to see Ella come into her own and find what she wants to do. I know Jason will move heaven and Earth to make it happen.

Riley is pregnant and looks ready to pop any time, but still has a few months to go. Blaze is so protective of her. I watch as he rubs her feet as they sit on the swing and talk with Jason and Ella.

I love it here and the family that surrounds me. I am grateful every day for Sage barging her way in and giving me all of this, but I can't help but feel like something is missing. It's because *someone* is missing, but I am the only one who knows it.

I've been texting Sarah on and off all day and I texted her when we pulled into town, but I haven't gotten anything back. I know she is busy, but I hope I can see her tonight. I don't want to waste any time with her.

"It's great being here with family, isn't it?" Mom says as she sits down and pulls me from my thoughts.

"Yeah." I force a smile and try not to let her see how distracted I am.

"Your turn will come, and soon. I feel it." Mom has always been able to read us pretty well.

I look at her but don't say anything. I know she doesn't need an answer.

"It's a gut feeling I have as a mom. You don't have to tell me anything, but if she is it for you, fight for her and don't back down. Don't let her friend-zone you like Megan tried to do with Hunter. Push her. Then next summer you could be here with her, our family complete. Well, until we start adding all those grandbabies."

She pats my knee and stands up just as my phone pings. I take a deep breath and send up a silent prayer it's her.

Sarah: Sorry working a shift at the diner and we just finished our lunch rush. I hope you made it into town OK!

What the hell is she doing working at the diner?

She busted her ass to get her degree in education so she can be an elementary school teacher, her dream job, and she is working in some small-town diner?

No way.

Not happening on my watch.

Mom's words are still fresh in my mind.

Push.

That's just what I plan to do. I hope she is ready because I plan to not just push her to reach her own dreams but to push her to be mine as well. There has to be a way I can make both happen.

I can't get the picture of all of us here next year with a few nieces and nephews running around and Sarah in my arms, out of my head.

Seven years is long enough to wait.

Me: Perfect, I'm starving. I'm going to head your way in a few.

I may have just eaten lunch with my family and Ella's chicken salad sandwiches were amazing. But if spending time with Sarah means eating lunch again then you better believe I am eating a second lunch.

Chapter 2

Sarah

I blow the hair out of my face as I see Mac's text that he is on his way here. Just great. I knew I'd have to have this conversation with him when he was here, I was just hoping it could wait until right before he left.

My luck isn't that good, as the last few months have shown me. I bust my butt to get my teaching degree. I have always wanted to be an elementary school teacher. I just love kids and want to work with them all day, and then hand them back to their parents at night and go home to a quiet house drink some wine and watch some Outlander. It's like being a grandparent. You spoil the kids, teach them, play with them, then send them home, break out a bottle of wine, and relax. That sounds like heaven for me. I also want to do some virtual teaching and was able to take a few courses in that as well.

My whole plan was that I could work anywhere with this degree. I do mean anywhere because I don't have to stay in Walker Lake. I love the few friends I have, like Sky, but I have to get away from my parents. I'm twenty-two and they are still so damn controlling. It doesn't help that I had to move back in with them after graduating.

Mac doesn't know all that though, he just knows my dream is to teach and how much I love the kids.

The bell over the door goes off and I jump up, but it's not him. An older gentleman sits down in Jenna's section. Jenna and I have become good friends since I started working here. She is a year older than me but plans to stay in Walker Lake with her family.

Jenna's family is new to town and they are great people. Her dad is some business tycoon who built a huge company and now is retired and just collecting income from the business. The great thing is, you would never know they are rich just meeting them on the street. Her whole family is very down to earth. Their house is amazing, right on the lake, and their family has lots of love to give.

Jenna has a very exotic look with chiseled features, tan skin, and dark brown hair. She has been approached to model several times but wasn't interested. If she had taken them up on it, I bet she'd have one hell of a career. Right now, she is writing a book. Her parents support her, and she took the job at the diner to meet people in town and because her character is a waitress and she wanted to immerse herself. I always find her making notes in a notebook every free chance she has.

She has one of those picture-perfect families, kind of like the Walton's where they are all close-knit and care about each other. Kind of like Mac's family.

Jenna walks in from taking the guy's order.

"Hey, cover me for five minutes? I'm going to head into the bathroom and fix myself up."

"Oh, is the mysterious Mac coming in?" she jokes.

"Actually, yes, so play nice."

She holds her hands up. "Always. I can't wait to meet him. So, hurry and get ready."

I rush off to the bathroom out the back and look in the mirror. 'Not too bad,' I think; at least there are no stains on my clothes. I pull my hair out of the messy bun and run my fingers through it before tying it back up in a neater messy bun. I splash some water on my face. I didn't wear any makeup today and I'm kicking myself for it but there is nothing I can do about that now. As I'm drying my face, there's a knock at the door.

"I'll be out in a minute," I call out.

"It's me," Jenna calls. "I've got some makeup, figured you're regretting not putting any on today."

I open the door and take the makeup bag. "You are a lifesaver. Thank you. Thank you. Thank you. I owe you one."

"You owe me nothing, but maybe lunch one day this week."

"Deal!" I close the door and open the bag. I swipe on some eyeliner, eye shadow, and mascara. The first lip gloss I put on isn't my shade, so I wipe it off but the second one is more subtle and looks good. I head out and hand Jenna the bag.

"Take a deep breath, Sarah, it's just Mac," she says.

Just Mac, if only she knew.

Jenna knows Mac as my best guy friend who I have a little crush on. She doesn't know that the reason I don't date is because I compare everything a guy does to what Mac does. She doesn't know the reason I am still a virgin is because the thought of kissing or sleeping with any guy that isn't Mac makes me feel sick. She also doesn't know that I will never tell him any of this.

There is no way he feels the same about me. I mean, Mac is gorgeous. Over the years his muscles have filled out from all the ranch work he does. The way his Wranglers hug the curves of his ass should be illegal. His tan skin is dark from his Native American roots; it has me itching to touch it every time I am near him. He wears his black hair a little long, but most don't know that because of the cowboy hat he wears which covers it.

Jenna also doesn't know how a thousand butterflies launch in my stomach every time his eyes lock with mine, or how a simple touch sends sparks straight to my core. I can't tell her any of this because she will try to push us together and there is no way a sexy cowboy like him will want anything romantic to do with me. Besides, he is the last thing I need while I try to get a job and get out of this town.

Back home I'm sure he'd be seeing someone he hasn't mentioned or maybe he plays the field. We don't talk about our love lives and I never ask because I couldn't stand to hear him talk about another girl.

"So, if Mac is in town that means his family is too, right?"

"Yeah, they're in town for the week."

"Will you be spending a lot of time with them?" Jenna asks.

"Yes, don't be mad I'm ditching you a few days."

"Oh, that's not what I'm worried about, does he have any hot brothers?"

I laugh. "Three of them, but sadly for you, they're all married now."

"Dang, a girl can hope to snag a hot cowboy."

"There is something to be said about those cowboy muscles, they are something to look at when they are swimming in the lake."

Jenna squeals. "Okay, now you have to take me with you, I need some eye candy. Please!"

"I'll talk to Mac." I laugh.

The bell dings and Jenna takes the guy's food out to him and comes back.

"So what's his family like?"

"They actually remind me of your family. Very down to Earth and all-round great people."

Jenna nods and the bell over the door goes off again.

Chapter 3

Mac

I park in front of the diner and take a look down the street. Megan says the town of Walker Lake reminds her of that town from the show Gilmore Girls, Sleepy Hollow but on a lake. She made me watch with her a few times to show me and I tend to agree.

The downtown is set up like a square with a courthouse in the middle. The diner, shops, a bar, the library, and some offices surround the courthouse. The whole town has a very relaxed waterfront lakeside vibe that screams more mountain fresh air and less Texas heat.

They have all sorts of events and decorate up for the fall and Christmas. Plus they do a huge July 4th parade, a BBQ festival, a bake-off, and more every year. Mom and Dad always say if they ever leave the ranch, this is where they would move to, but let's be real, they will never leave the ranch. They will be buried there like the rest of us.

I look up at the diner. Sarah worked here after school until she left for college. Sometimes she would have a shift when I'd come to visit, and I'd hang out at a back table and watch her so we could talk between customers.

She has such a friendly personality; you can't help but be drawn to her. Everyone loves her. I've seen her put a smile on someone even on their worst day and she has put more smiles on my own face than I can count. I hate that she is working back here again. I feel like it's her taking a big step backward and I need to find out why. Why she is working here and why she didn't tell me?

Once I know why I can help her fix it. I know she won't accept my help outright, but that doesn't mean I can't work behind the scenes to help her out. Like last year when she got a flat tire, she was stressed about paying for it but needed her car to get to class. I found out where she took the car to and paid the bill for her anonymously, though I'm sure she knew it was me, she played along like she didn't have a clue.

I take a deep breath and head into the diner. The bell rings as the door opens and my eyes scan the room before they land on her coming out from the kitchen with that big smile on her face that drew me to her all those years ago.

"Hey, sunshine." I smile and walk over to her. Even in her waitress uniform and apron with her hair in a messy knot on top of her head, she is still the most beautiful girl I have ever seen. That beauty has only grown over the years and has been the star of many of my sexy dreams.

I push my luck just a bit and pull her into a full hug, pressing her against my chest. Before today we would do those friendly side hugs, but I decided on the way over here to push. I plan to show her how she should be treated and how she would be treated if she was mine.

At the very least, I need to set the bar extremely high for any guy who might try to win her over. That's what I tell myself, but the thought of another guy with her just makes my stomach churn. I'm thankful she has never mentioned any of the guys she has dated because I couldn't take it. I'm sure she has to have dated; she is fucking gorgeous and has a heart as big as her dreams. Some guy is going to be lucky to settle down with her and I can't think about the fact that it won't be me.

She lays her head on my chest and wraps her arms around my waist. I rest my head on top of her head, close my eyes, and just take her in. The sea salt scent she says comes from the spray she puts in her hair, mixes with the honeysuckle from her shampoo, and it's the most calming scent in the world to me. When she pulls back, I notice the other waitress, a woman our age, standing in the kitchen doorway smiling.

I look back at Sarah. "Where is your section?"

She points to the left side of the diner and I take a seat in the corner where I will be able to see her as much as possible. It's also a smaller table, so won't take away from paying customers; I have no plans to leave anytime soon.

Both Sarah and the other waitress are whispering by the kitchen and it makes me smile, knowing they are talking about me. I look over the menu which hasn't changed much. They do rotate out a few seasonal dishes and desserts every few months.

Sarah and the other waitress then make their way over to my table.

"This is my friend Jenna. I've told her about you, and she wanted to meet you in person," Sarah says.

I smile and shake her hand. "Nice to meet you, Jenna."

"Nice to put a face to the name, though not exactly what I was expecting."

"Jenna!" Sarah hisses at her, making Jenna laugh.

"What exactly were you expecting?"

"I don't know, a white t-shirt and jeans with mud on them?"

"The cowboy stereotype? If you visit on the ranch you're likely to see that, but I'm on vacation so I break out my nicer clothes."

"These clothes work too."

Jenna shrugs then turns and heads back to the kitchen leaving Sarah and me alone.

"She seems fun," I joke.

"She's new to town. Well, newer. Her family has been here for about a year now, but she is fun to be around, and working with her is entertaining."

"Speaking of..." I look at her more seriously. "Why didn't you mention you were working here before now?"

She shrugs her shoulders. "It didn't come up. Now, what can I get you?"

"You mean I didn't specifically ask you if you were working at the diner again? Gee, sorry I didn't ask, and I'll have the BLT, extra fries."

This is my standing order. I always get the extra fries because she likes to snack on them while she's working. Often she doesn't get to eat until after her shift and I like to feed her and make sure she isn't hungry.

She turns to walk off, but I grab her hand and gently tug her back. I look at her hand in mine for a minute before looking back at her.

"Sunshine, I'm not mad, I just wish you had told me. Go put the food order in then come back and tell me what's going on," I say in a soft voice. She nods and I let go of her hand and watch her walk back to the kitchen.

She brings me back out a sweet tea knowing without even having to ask what I want to drink. Seeing as there is only one other person in the diner, I think now is a good time to talk.

"Can you sit down for a minute?" I ask.

She looks around and then perches on the edge of the booth like she is uncomfortable.

"Just for a minute, the boss showed up while I was getting your drink."

"Tell me what's going on. No secrets, Sunshine, not between us."

She smiles then takes a deep breath.

"I've been applying to jobs like crazy, but nothing has come in. They all want experience and having no place to go I moved home, and things... well, they're not great but they aren't charging me rent or anything. I took this job to save money."

"Oh, Sunshine, I wish you'd said something to me. You always have a place to go with me, you understand that, right?" I watch her as she nods and I look at her properly. She seems tired, stressed maybe.

"What do you mean that things are not great at home?"

She looks out the window behind us like she is trying to gather her thoughts.

"We aren't seeing eye to eye right now. A teacher's job is beneath them, but they forced me into this job. I've just been avoiding them at this point. Less we talk, less we fight."

I hate that she is in that kind of environment. I've only met her parents a few times and they never seemed to like me, but the feeling was mutual.

"Why don't you pack a bag and come stay with my family at the lake house this week. I know they want to see you and we have plenty of room. A break will do you, and them, some good."

"I don't know, Mac."

"You'd be spending a lot of time at the lake anyway. Why not stay? There's an office you can use to apply for jobs all day if you want. Just close the door no one but me will bother you." I get a hint of a smile from her there.

"Okay, I have two more hours on my shift," she says as the bell in the kitchen dings.

"Well, I'm not going anywhere, I'm a slow eater, after all."

She smiles at me, but the smile is wiped away when another voice fills the diner.

"Let's go, Sarah, you're here to work, not chit chat." I glance at the man who looks to be in his forties. He's dressed in nice pants and a polo shirt that shows his belly that hangs over his belt by a good six inches.

The man's eyes follow Sarah as she goes to get my food from the kitchen, and she gives him a wide berth as she walks around him. I don't like the way his eyes track her, and it's obvious he's staring at her ass as she walks by. Something about this guy seems off.

She brings me my food and her expression is blank.

"Who's that?" I nod my head toward the guy.

"That's Lee, he's my boss."

"Sarah..."

She shakes her head. "Not here. We can talk tonight, okay?"

I nod and look back at him, he still hasn't taken his eyes off her. Jenna heads over to bring the other gentleman in the diner his check and Lee doesn't even give her a second glance.

I had already planned to stay until the end of her shift but there is no way I am leaving now.

Chapter 4

Sarah

Of course, Lee has to show up now, something else Mac will want to talk about. He picked up on how uncomfortable Lee makes me feel from the start. I knew he would, he can read me like a book.

Lee has never done anything to me. He's strict and can be a bit rude, but it's more the vibe I get from him, the way I catch him looking at me that makes me uneasy.

I keep an eye on him while I do my side work and every time I pass his table, I sneak a French fry off Mac's plate and he smiles. I'm refilling the salt and pepper shakers getting ready for the dinner rush when Lee walks up to me.

"Who is that guy?" he asks, cocking his head toward Mac. I'm not a liar normally, but something in my gut tells me not to tell him the truth. So I go for a different version of the truth.

"His family is friends with Beth."

Beth is the owner of the diner and is Lee's boss. It's true, his family is friends with her, they have been coming to this town for almost ten years from what I understand. Back then, Beth ran the place herself. Once I went away to college, she hired Lee so she could semi-retire.

My parents are friends with Lee, and I have a feeling they talk about me often because he knows things about me that I've never told him and it's just creepy.

He stands a bit straighter, seeming nervous. "How long does he plan to stay here?" I wonder if he thinks Beth sent Mac here to spy on him. Wouldn't that be nice?

I shrug my shoulders. "I never ask, but he normally stays a bit. When he's in town he likes to hang out here to get away from his family, there's a lot of them."

He nods and looks over at Mac who is watching us now.

"Guess I should go introduce myself."

"Guess you should. I need to finish refilling these anyway." I nod toward the shakers.

He straightens his shoulders again and walks over to Mac, holding out his hand.

"Hello, I'm Lee, the general manager here. I wanted to come over and introduce myself. I haven't seen you in here before."

"I know who you are." Mac looks at Lee's hand but his southern manners his mama taught him win out. "I'm Mac." He reluctantly shakes Lee's hand.

"Well, can I clear this plate for you?"

"No." Mac's response is simple but firm. He finished his sandwich long ago, but we have both been snacking on the fries.

Lee shifts his weight, clearly uncomfortable now and I take the tray and start replacing the salt and pepper shakers on the empty tables. Lee mumbles something then heads back to his office.

I walk over and switch out the shakers at Mac's table and smile at him.

"What did you say to him before he came over?"

"He asked who you were, I told him that your family is friends with Beth." I shrug my shoulders and watch him smile.

• • • • • • • • • •

After work, Mac follows me to my parent's place and I'm thankful that they're not home.

I pack a bag while he waits in his car then I follow him over to his family's lake house in my car. I know how to get there, I've been there so many times, but I like that he wants to make sure I get there okay.

Every summer when his family is here, I spend all my free time at the lake house with him, and many times Sky would join us. The days would be filled with swimming and the nights by the campfire with smores.

At least once a year we would have a camp-out and pitch a tent near the lake under the stars. Those nights are some of my favorites just staying up all night talking. Megan, Sage, and I bonded, being the only girls in the group back then. We would do girls' nights getting our nails done and Megan would practice doing our hair and makeup.

His sisters were the ones I was with when I tried alcohol for the first time at the age of seventeen, they were there to help me with my all-grown-up college wardrobe, and to teach me how to cook. His brothers also beat up some guy who wouldn't leave me alone in my senior year of high school. If I didn't think too hard, it was easy to imagine them as my family. It's all I have ever wanted.

I was bummed I hadn't been able to make it to the weddings this year. Blaze married Riley during midterms and Sage and Colt got married during finals. I was dealing with my parents and moving when Hunter and Megan got married, and just recently I tried to make it to Jason and Ella's wedding, but I couldn't get time off. I was going to go anyway but the hissy fit my mother threw caused me to stay in town.

I felt so bad missing the weddings because they have always accepted me with open arms and Mac has been by my side supporting me and cheering me on all that time. He took me out for my 21st birthday and let me crash at the lake house after I got drunk. He has always been my designated driver when I needed one. I smile at this as we pull into the driveway.

Before I can even get my car turned off, he's there and opening my door for me and grabbing my bag in one hand and my hand in his other. This is new, we've never held hands before. He also has never hugged me like he did when he saw me at the diner today.

I like having my hand in his. I like that my hand fits as though it was meant to be there. I know it wasn't but in this moment in time, I can pretend.

We walk in and to the right is the staircase leading to the loft. To the left is the main family room with the logwood walls you see in old wood cabins. A huge stone fireplace and large window doors that fold open overlooking the back with the lake view. This space runs the length of the house as it flows into the dining room and kitchen down to a small hallway with an office, guest bath, and ending at the master bedroom at the far end of the house.

This has always been my favorite part, we would move the dining table out of the way and run and see how far we could slide in our socks. There were a few sliced foreheads when someone ran into a wall. I have a scar on my left shoulder from landing on the dining room table, but it was all so much fun.

To the right are different hallways leading to Mac's brothers and sisters' rooms and then there is a full finished walkout basement downstairs with more rooms, a bunk room, a game room, and a small theater room.

"Hey, everyone," Mac calls out and I hear Helen, Mac's mom, yell back.

"On the deck!"

Mac pulls me to his room and sets the bag on his bed.

"I figured you can stay here with me and I can take the couch." He nods towards the couch that is big enough to be a bed and I nod.

He takes my hand again and we head out to the deck where I can smell the grill and hear everyone talking.

"Hey, you guys all remember Sarah? Ella, this is Sarah. Ella is Jason's wife, they're here celebrating their honeymoon and were crazy enough to invite us all out to spend the week with them."

I lift my hand and give them a short wave.

"Hey." I smile.

"Sarah is going to be staying with us while we are here. I figured she can have my bed and I'll take the couch."

"Oh, no, I'm much smaller, I'll take the couch."

Helen chuckles and looks at my hand in Mac's and smiles.

"You won't win this one, dear. His manners won't let you take the couch."

I just shake my head because I know she is right.

After dinner is my favorite part of spending time with Mac's family. They get a game of cards going and those who aren't playing just sit and talk and there is so much laughter.

After losing twice to a game of Bullshit, I step out and let Ella take my place. Jason has been teaching it to her. I join Mac on the porch swing, and he puts his hand on the back of the swing and pats the space next to him for me to join him. I sit down beside him.

"Feet up," he says, and I rest my feet on the swing so I'm sitting sideways and have my back leaning against him as he slowly starts rocking us.

"I was sitting out here earlier when we first got in and I had this feeling that something was missing. It was you. You were missing, because now it feels complete."

I smile and think about that.

"I always feel at home here with your family. I feel more a part of the family than I do around my own parents."

He kisses the top of my head. Another first.

"You will always be welcome here and safe here. I hope you know that."

"I do." I smile at him.

"When do you have another shift at the diner?"

"I have the next two days off."

"Why don't you invite Jenna over to hang out. Is Sky in town?"

"She is, actually, visiting her parents."

"Why don't you invite them over you can hang out with the girls tomorrow, I heard them making plans."

"I'd like that if you are sure it's okay."

"Of course it is."

We spend most of the evening there swinging and watching his family and just soaking in each other's company.

Chapter 5

Mac

As we get ready for bed, I let her use the bathroom first. When I come out from my turn, she is standing in the middle of the room in a pair of sleep shorts and one of my old Kenny Chaney t-Shirts.

"I knew you stole that shirt!"

She blushes. "I wanted a piece of you at school with me."

I instantly soften. "I look good on you," I smirk at her making her blush even more.

"Really, I can take the couch. It's going to be so uncomfortable, you being so big and all. You aren't going to fit."

"Oh, Sunshine, I will fit. We will just take it nice and slow."

"I... um..."

I chuckle at how flustered she is. She is so damn sexy when I get her off balance like this with the blush on her cheeks. I have to walk over to the couch and turn my back to her to hide how hard it makes me. I try to adjust myself, but it's no use.

"I promise I will be okay and fit just fine."

I start to make up the couch expecting her to climb into bed but when I turn around, she is still standing in the middle of the room.

"What is it, Sunshine?"

"Well, the bed is so big, why don't we just share it? We are grown adults, after all."

I look her up and down with her tan legs exposed, her shorts just barely cover her lush ass cheeks that I just want to dig my fingers into. Even from this side of the room, I can tell she isn't wearing a bra under my shirt. I can see the stiff peaks of her nipples and I'm glad I'm not the only one turned on as hell right now.

"We don't have to..."

"I promise it's okay, Mac."

I look her over again and nod, grabbing my pillow and heading toward the bed.

We climb into bed and both hug our own sides. The lights are off but there is enough glow from the moon and the night light in the bathroom that I can see her face when I look over at her.

I turn on my side and she does the same. I study her and without saying a word I reach out and take her hand in mine in the middle of the bed. I run my fingers over her palm, stretching her hand open before laying my hand on hers and intertwining our fingers.

When I look back at her she is looking at our hands in wonder and I hope I'm not pushing my luck.

Her eyes lock with mine and for a minute neither of us speaks but I have questions that need to be answered.

"Why didn't you tell me about working at the diner?"

She is quiet for a moment, lost in thought.

"Don't you ever get tired of being my cheerleader?"

"Never."

"I just... you seem to believe more in me than I do myself some days. I felt that by taking the job at the diner I was letting you down somehow. I know it doesn't make sense, but I just did."

"Sunshine... I am proud of you as a person. You are kind, sweet, full of life, and when you put your mind to something, you do it. Working at the diner is just a path to what you want. When we were looking to expand the ranch and buy Sage's family's land, we all worked our butts off. I flipped burgers at the cafe in town, cleaned bathrooms at the gas station, and helped clean Jason's bar. All of which had nothing to do with ranching but allowed me to help save money for the bigger goal. That's what you are doing now, saving money for a bigger goal. Now tell me what's going on with your parents."

"They didn't think I was serious about getting a teaching degree and they never paid enough attention to realize I was really doing it until I graduated. A daughter as a teacher just isn't good enough for them. They're friends with Lee and stress how they've pulled so many strings to get me the job when I know all I had to do was call Beth and she'd have had him hire me on the spot. Now they're holding the job over my head and I just feel trapped."

"Well, let's hope this time apart will clear their heads."

"Yeah, they aren't happy that I'm here. I texted them when we got here, and they demanded I come home and how dare I take time off to spend with you and your family. I told them to leave me alone and then turned my phone off."

"I'm sorry, Sunshine. I know a thing or two about shitty parents. You know I'm here for you no matter what, no matter where, no matter what time of day. Right?"

She nods.

I still want to talk about her boss, but I feel like we have covered enough ground tonight, so I'm going to let it be.

I gently reach out and push some hair away from her face and tuck it behind her ear, letting my fingers trail along her jaw line softly before tracing her lips and then pulling away. I hear her breathing pick up and I reach up to take her hand back.

"I was thinking of staying here for another week after the family heads home. Will you stay with me?"

I wasn't planning on it, but the idea popped into my head and out of my mouth before I could stop it. Now I'm praying she says yes because I want nothing more than a week with her here at the lake house, just the two us.

"My parents won't like that."

"Screw your parents, I can handle them. What do *you* want?"

She's quiet for a minute and I worry that I've pushed too hard. My heart is racing and I'm going over every argument in the book if she tries to say no. When I hear her reply, my world stops.

"I want to stay here with you."

"Then you will, and I will handle everything else. Okay?"

She nods and the need to hold her is so strong I think I might die if I don't get my arms around her.

"Can I hold you?" My voice is hoarse as I whisper.

"Yes."

The sweetest sound in the world. I hold my arm out and she scoots over and presses her chest up against my side and rests her head on my shoulder. I'm in sweatpants and a t-shirt but the heat from her body still penetrates as if there is nothing between us.

I lay there soaking up the feeling of her in my arms for so long that her breathing evens out. The last time I remember looking at the clock before I drift off too is 3:00 a.m.

Chapter 6

Sarah

I love soaking up the sun on the lake. It's been one of my favorite things to do since I was a kid, and Mac's sisters do it right! They have tied eight tube floats together in a circle around a floating cooler and we are all tied to the dock.

We have been out here for an hour now soaking up the sun and watching the guys play whatever sports game they've invented. Even having Mac's mom out here has been fun and Jenna and Sky seem to be getting along with everyone really well, too.

"So, how is newlywed life?" I ask Ella. Her parents are super conservative, so she and Jason were always chaperoned when they were together; they didn't even share their first kiss until their wedding day, from what Mac told me.

"Oh, I love it! I know this is still the honeymoon, but it's been perfect. I love my family, but for the first time I can find out who I want to be, and Jason is so supportive."

"How was it adjusting from always having a chaperone to having alone time?" Jenna asks.

"Honestly, we, ugh..." She blushes, making us all laugh.

"You didn't even notice at first, did you?" Megan jokes.

"No. It was actually on the drive here that it hit me."

"Did the outfit we bought you do what you wanted?" Sage asks.

Ella's face turns bright red.

"Oh my God! Now you have to tell us!" Sky squeals.

"Before the wedding, Ella here asked for a sisters' shopping trip, she wanted to get some contraband clothes." Riley smiles

Jenna and Sky both wear matching confused looks so Ella opens her mouth to explain but Helen speaks first.

"I don't know if this is something I want to hear." She reaches for another beer and all the girls break out laughing.

"Well, my parents insisted on very modest clothing, sleeves, a high neckline, dresses, or skirts that were no higher than my knees. No pants, but leggings under the dresses or skirts were allowed. Oh, and the swimsuits were horrible I looked at least thirty pounds heavier in them! So, I asked to go shopping in Dallas. We bought jeans, shorts, some tops, and this swimsuit." She gestures towards her swimsuit that reminds me of a 1950's pin up model.

"And..." Megan urges her on and her face turns even redder if that is possible.

She mumbles something but no one hears her.

"What was that?" Jenna teases with a big smile on her face.

"An outfit for under my wedding dress."

"You go, girl!" Jenna Sky claps their hands and Sky splashes her feet in the water. I can't help the big smile on my face.

"Did he just lose his mind?" Sky has always been the one to push the envelope.

"Things a mother doesn't need to know..." Helen tries to cover her ears.

"Oh, Mom, you keep asking for grandbabies, this is how grandbabies are made!" Sage giggles.

"I don't need the details, just the babies." Helen chugs half of her beer and we all laugh.

"Well?" Riley looks at Ella.

Ella just nods all shy and everyone claps again.

It takes a few minutes for everyone to calm down and then eyes turn to me.

"So, you and Mac?" Sage asks.

"Oh hush, Sage, let them be," her mom scolds.

"What? We all saw him holding her hand. He never does that, he never brings girls home, so I'm just wondering."

"Oh, we're just friends." I manage to get out, but my mind is racing. He doesn't hold hands or bring girls home? Does that mean he's a player and sleeps around or he just doesn't bring girls home to his family? I want to press and ask questions, but as this is his family it just doesn't seem right.

"Oh, girl, don't fall into that trap. I thought that for so long. I pushed Hunter away when he was the best thing to ever happen to me," Megan chimes in.

"Whoa, rewind. What happened?" Jenna looks at Sage.

"Yes, we haven't been given these details," Sky joins in.

Helen looks at me. "I tried, but I'm outnumbered now." She laughs.

"Well, Mac walks in with Sarah here last night," Sage starts.

"After her shift at the diner..." Jenna adds.

"He had a packed bag he takes to his room and then walks out on the deck holding her hand," Sage continues.

I rest my head on the back of the float and tilt my face toward the sun and close my eyes. I know from experience there is no point in trying to tell my side until they are done.

"Then he says that she is staying with us while we are here," Riley adds.

"After dinner, we played some cards then she steps out and goes and snuggles up on the porch swing with Mac and they stayed there laughing and whispering all night," Sage fills in.

I inwardly cringe, I love these girls even when they get like this. It's all fun and games until you are on this side of it.

"Hunter said he went to wake them up and let them know breakfast was ready this morning and they were asleep in the same bed, all snuggled up together."

"Megan!" I squeal.

"What? Is it not true? Did my husband lie to me?"

I sigh. "It's true. BUT..."

They all start talking at once and I can't keep up.

"I knew they were together."

"After all these years, it's so romantic."

"I bet this is why he never dates."

"Mac has loved her for years; I've seen it in the way he looks at her."

"You know she is always talking about him at work." Jenna gives everyone a knowing look.

I have to stop this.

"STOP! It was only because he was going to sleep on the couch, and have you seen him? He's huge, he wouldn't have fit. I couldn't let him."

"But that doesn't explain why you two were all cuddled up this morning...?" Jenna lets her question hang with a raised eyebrow.

"It must have happened while we slept," I mumble, hoping the heat I'm feeling on my face is the sun.

There are a few snickers from around the circle, but we hear the guys start yelling so we give them our attention only to find them all with their shirts off.

"Damn, you sure you don't have a few more brothers locked up for us poor girls over here?" Jenna asks.

"Sorry, but they sure are nice to look at, aren't they?" Riley says.

"They sure are. I'm sorry I don't mean to be creeping on your husbands and all."

"You can look, but no touching," Sage says, and everyone agrees.

Sage catcalls at the guys causing them all to turn around and grin at us.

"We are trying to see the show and can't do that with your backs to us!" Sage yells.

Mac's eyes lock with mine and he winks at me and laughs with the guys.

"Would you like us to sit on the dock for your eye candy pleasure?" Colt calls back.

"Yes please!" Jenna yells and we all agree.

The guys all grab a beer then come and sit on the edge of the dock.

"What are we talking about, ladies?" Blaze asks.

Mac is watching me with a smirk on his face like he knows the answer already.

"Well, you guys, of course!" Riley yells back causing everyone to laugh. We sit and talk like this for another hour until it's time for lunch and the guys help us all out of the lake.

· · · ● · ● · ● · ·

The last two days have flown by. I love being around his family and there has always been something about this lake house that has been so relaxing. I turned my phone back on because Jenna and Sky made me before they left. It flooded with texts from not only my parents, but also from Lee saying he heard I disappeared and that I had better show up for my shift.

What the hell?

Jenna made me promise to tell Mac what was going on, but since we hadn't talked about Lee, I didn't know how to bring it up.

We still continue to sleep in the same bed, snuggled up together every night and have spent the last few days just hanging out swimming in the lake, or circled up on the couch together in the media room watching TV.

Now I'm getting ready for work. I sent Lee a simple text that night saying he had heard wrong and I would be in. I ignored him after that. Mac walks in as I'm putting on my make-up and comes up behind me. I look at him in the mirror for a minute before he speaks.

"You don't need any of that, you are beautiful, Sunshine."

"I make better tips when I wear makeup."

He takes a deep breath and shakes his head.

"Can I drive you to work and pick you up? I was thinking maybe we can catch a movie after your shift. It's been a while since I saw a movie. Anything you want, your choice."

"Anything?" I smile and lean against the counter.

"Anything." He nods and crosses his arms over his chest.

"So if I want to go see the Gone With the Wind they are replaying this week, you would go?"

He nods. "And sit through all four hours with you."

I laugh. "Actually, I would love to see something more of a comedy."

"Done. Don't fill up on food at the diner, we'll get all the bad-for-you movie food."

"I'd like that. I'll bring some clothes, so I don't smell like greasy diner food."

He smiles. "If you want, but I love the smell of the diner on you."

I crinkle my nose. "You're weird."

On the way to the diner, he holds my hand and we talk about what movies are out and decide on the new rom com with the girl from Pitch Perfect.

He walks me to the diner door. "I'll be here a bit before your shift ends, call or text me and I can always come early."

"I will, it's a weeknight so I think it will be a slow shift."

He leans in to kiss me on the cheek.

"Have a good shift, Sunshine."

I watch him walk back to the truck with a smile on my face.

I walk in to find Lee watching the whole thing from the kitchen door. "Why is he bringing you to work?"

I tense. Is he kidding me?

"None of your business."

"It is my business when I'm told my employee has disappeared and I don't even know if she is showing up for work."

Yet again he has been talking to my parents, prying into my private life on things that are none of his business. This isn't normal, this isn't ok.

"Still none of your business, and my parents are spreading rumors and lies. I told you I'd be here. I am an adult and I make my own choices and I suggest you drop it." I stare him down.

I've had about enough of this. I need this job, I need to save money, but I think it's time to start looking for something else. I can't work for Lee anymore. I turn on my heel and head to the kitchen to start my shift.

Chapter 7

Mac

When I drop Sarah off at the diner, I can tell she doesn't want to go in. As much I would like to think it's because of the amazing two days we've spent together, a part of me knows there is something more.

Now I'm kicking myself for not bringing up her boss again and putting it off. When she walks in, I hang out just on the other side of the window where they can't see me, but I can hear them, and I don't like what I do hear.

I can't let her keep working there, but I know she won't quit just because I ask her to. I also get the feeling that it will cause more tension with her parents if she quits.

I spend the next hour driving around the lake, thinking of my options, and once I have a plan, I head back to the house to talk to everyone. When I pull up in the driveway, I send off a mass text asking everyone to meet me on the deck.

When I walk in, everyone is there, and they look concerned.

"What's going on, Mac?" Mom asks.

"Let's sit down, I need to talk to you about something."

I go on and tell them about the vibes I got from Sarah's boss the other day and what I overheard today.

"I'm kicking myself for not bringing her boss back up and not making her talk about it, but she told me a bit about her parents and it seems when she didn't get a job right out of school she had no choice but to move back in with them. So, without thinking, I invited her to stay here with me for a week after you guys leave, is that okay?"

"Oh, of course, son. This house is just as much yours as anyone else's here," Dad says.

"Sage, would you be willing to ride back with Mom and Dad and let me borrow your truck?"

"It's yours."

"Now for the big favor."

"Whatever it is, you know the answer is yes, right?" Blaze asks and I nod.

"I was wondering if we can move Sarah in here so she can get away from her parents. Once that happens, I think I can get her to quit that job."

"Well, this is perfect timing. We got a call today that the woman we have come in and clean the place has retired, so we need someone to clean it when we leave. There are some light decorating projects we wanted to have tackled as well. Mostly painting and replacing some furniture and getting the place ready for grandbabies. We'd be happy to pay her."

My eyes mist over. This is what this family does all the time. They will help anyone and give them the shirt off their back, if you only ask.

"I have one more idea."

"Let's hear it," Megan says.

"Well, she has been having trouble finding a job she can use her degree with. I was thinking you guys keep wanting to set up a schoolroom on the ranch and hire more help. With more people getting married I'm sure more babies will be on the way. I know Sage has been putting off getting someone to help around the house with cooking and cleaning, maybe we can hire her? I know some of the ranch hands would love to be able to have the option for the kids to do schoolwork on the ranch and not head into town every day."

"Well, now's as good a time as any. There is one more baby on the way," Megan announces.

Everyone jumps up and starts hugging her and rubbing her belly, making her laugh. Mom insists on several side by side pictures of her and Riley even though Megan doesn't have a bump yet.

Once everyone calms down, Sage looks at me.

"Sage, she is it for me. If I don't get her out to the ranch, my options are to leave the ranch and follow her... or lose her."

Sage's eyes soften before she looks around at everyone nodding their heads.

"Well, I've had the budget set aside to bring someone in to take over the house duties. Can she cook for us plus the ranch hands, Mac? That can be 30 people on a busy day."

"Sage you are the best teacher out there. She is a good cook we all know that. Few adjustments and she will do fine."

"It looks like we all agree. Tell us what we need to do to get her there because losing you isn't an option and you losing her isn't an option either."

"Let me talk to her tonight and I will let you know. We are going to see a movie when she gets out of work, maybe we will come sit on the dock when we get home and talk."

"Let us know when the movie ends, we'll hang out inside," Mom says.

"Son, what do you think of me calling Beth and letting her know what is going on with this Lee guy? I think I should. Who else is he preying on at the diner?" Dad makes a good point.

I know it's the right thing to do because someone will replace Sarah, and who's to say he won't try to move on to Jenna? I know Sarah would never forgive herself if that happened.

"Okay, please let me know what she says."

"Now go get ready for your date," Megan says.

"Not a date, just movies like we always do as friends."

Megan waves her hands at me. "Some hand holding and a kiss and it's a date."

I shake my head, stand up, and hug everyone and start making plans.

• • • • • • • • • •

I dress up just a bit more than our normal hanging-out clothes because Megan is right, I want this to be a date, but I'm scared to call it that. I leave early and head to the diner. She doesn't get out for another hour, but I thought I'd grab a drink and hang out. She texted earlier and said she had been busy all day, which is great for tips but not so great for her to grab even a snack.

I walk in and notice the place is pretty packed, but Jenna greets me right away. "Take that booth over there, it's her section." She points to the wall then delivers the drinks in her hands. I take it all in, but I don't see Sarah and with everything going on I know I won't rest until do.

A few minutes later she comes out of the kitchen with an annoyed look on her face and her eyes go wide when she sees me. I offer her a friendly smile and she gives me a forced smile back. I want to pull her from this place and tell anyone who put this look on her face to fuck off.

"Hey, you're early," she says.

"Thought I'd come in and wait for you."

She looks over her shoulder and sighs, Lee is watching us.

"Can I get you anything?"

"Sweet tea and some fries, please."

She smiles and nods and walks off to put my order in. I pull out my phone and text my dad.

Me: Did you get a hold of Beth?

Dad: No. Everything okay?

Me: She is stressed, and her boss is in her personal space and watching her like he owns her. I hate it.

Dad: Let me try Beth again.

Lee watches me but also watches Sarah. When she walks by to set my drink down, he grabs her arm right by her breast and I almost lose it. I have enough sense to snap a picture, since my phone is open, and I hear him say, "I need you to stay for the dinner shift."

She yanks her arm away and scowls. "I have plans."

"Not anymore, you don't," he says with a sneer.

She slams the glass on the counter then storms off into the kitchen. I text the photo to my family and say 'S.O.S'. They reply to say they are heading my way now. It's more muscle than I need but better safe than sorry. How I have any self-control is beyond me, because all I see is red and the need to rip his balls off.

Mom texts a few minutes later that Dad is on the phone with Beth now.

Sarah walks out of the kitchen with my fries and when she sets them down, I try to get her attention.

"Hey," I say in a soft voice.

When she looks up at me, I ask her, "Do you trust me? I mean like, trust me that I have a plan with what I'm about to do. Full on, head first, ask questions later kind of trust me?"

She frowns but then takes a deep breath.

"Yes," she replies, and I nod. My phone dings twice and she turns away before I can say anything else.

Mom: Beth is pissed, she had no idea.
Blaze: We are here.
Me: Come in and just be my back up.

A minute later the four of them are standing and blocking the door. Blaze, Colt, Hunter, and Jason are pure cowboy muscle and a force not to be messed with when it comes to what is theirs. Sarah is mine, even if she won't admit it, which makes her part of our family and we protect family.

I stand up and toss enough cash on the table to cover the cost of the order and when Sarah sees the guys and me, she stops. I walk over to her and put an arm around her waist, just as Lee's phone rings.

"My guess is that is Beth calling to fire you for sexual harassment in light of the lawsuit we will be filing. Come near Sarah again and I'll have your ass thrown in jail. Consider this her two-week notice, but she won't be back."

"You have no proof!" He's stupid enough to snarl.

"I have a diner full of people and a photo that says otherwise."

I turn to Sarah and try to keep my voice soft. "Come on, Sunshine. Do you have anything you need from the back?"

"No." I watch her cringe and a hint of red coat her cheeks. She is playing with the ring on her right hand which I know means her nerves are getting the best of her. Time to get her out of here.

The guys part as we near the door then surround us and follow us out to the truck.

I help her in. "Keep your head high until we get out of here," I whisper, holding her gaze so she knows I'm totally here for her, then run around to my side.

The guys wait until we pull out before getting in their truck and heading home. I pull into a little county park on the way to the lake house and cut the engine. When I look at her, she is shaking.

I send up a prayer of thanks for Blaze's bench seat and pull her to me and just hold her. She already has a bruise forming on her arm and it sends more waves of rage through me, but as soon as I hear her tears, a vice grips my heart.

"I've got you," I soothe as I pull her toward me.

"Y-you said y-you h-have a-a plan?" she asks between sobs.

"Yes, do you want to hear it now? Or we can go back to the house, I'm sure the guys are opening up the wet bar in the game room for us."

"I want to h-hear it," she says as she calms herself down.

"Well, plan number one is that we move you into the lake house so you are away from your parents. Part two of that plan is that Mom and Dad's housekeeper just retired so when we leave, they will pay you to clean the house from top to bottom. It's more than you would make in two weeks at the diner. Part three is they have some small paint projects and redecorating and getting the house ready for the grandbabies they want you to oversee. Also paid. What do you think?"

She is quiet and I see her mind working behind those tear-filled eyes.

"You said plan number one?"

"Yes well, plan number two is my favorite. Megan just announced they are pregnant, and Riley is due in a few months. They have been talking about setting up a schoolroom and homeschooling the kids on the ranch, not just the new babies but many of the ranch hands have families on the ranch and kids too. They will need a teacher... Until then, Sage needs someone to help with cooking meals and cleaning the house, grocery shopping that sort of thing. She keeps putting it off, but she really needs help and the gig comes with a room and board, a small apartment in the main house. We can set you up with a space in the schoolroom for you to do your online teaching until the kids start school, then we can make you an office in the guest room or set you up in one of the cabins. I know there are a few teachers in town ready to retire so we can look there too if you want."

She is quiet but has stopped crying.

"It's a lot to think about. How about I take you up on plan one for now and think about plan two?"

"Perfect, you can even keep applying for jobs, you will have access to the computer in the office even once we are gone. Now let's head home and talk to my dad, he did speak to Beth and I was serious about pressing charges. I won't tolerate anyone putting bruises on you, he's lucky he's still breathing."

Before I know what is happening, she leans over and kisses my cheek, and says, "Thank you, Mac, I've never had someone take care of me like this."

"Get used to it, Sunshine, because I'm not going anywhere."

I send up a silent vow that I will be able to protect her always no matter how far apart we are, and I will do a better job at it than I have been. It never should have gotten this far.

Chapter 8

Sarah

There is so much to think about that my head is spinning as I lay on the bed and listen to the water running in the bathroom as Mac gets ready for bed. I saw my arm in the mirror earlier and there is already a nasty bruise. Sage took several photos of it and they asked me to consider pressing charges and said that they would cover any attorney fees if I did. I agreed to sleep on it.

I think about Mac and his brothers showing up and taking care of me. How quickly they were there, no questions asked. That's the type of family I want. I turned off my phone before I even got back to the house with Mac. I know my parents will be going crazy and I don't want them to influence my decisions.

I am already dreading having to face them to go get my stuff and tell them I am moving out. Mac and his brothers all agreed to go with me to make the move fast and to protect me, should the need arise.

I hear the water turn off and the click of the light switch before the door opens. A moment later the bed dips and Mac lies down next to me. I don't even hesitate to scoot over and snuggle up into his arms like I have been every night since I've been here. Tonight, I need it even more than before and he seems to know this because he is holding me a bit tighter too.

We lie there in silence for a while as he slowly rubs his hand down my back. We are both lost in thought but he speaks first.

"What's on your mind, Sunshine?"

"I think I want to press charges."

"I want you to. I still don't know how I kept it together seeing his hands on you like that. I know I can't let him walk free."

I nod. "I also want to go tomorrow and get my stuff from my parents' place and get it over with. I'm not turning my phone on until then, so it will be a shit show."

I can feel him smiling as he places a kiss on the top of my head.

"Won't be the first one I've had to deal with."

Mac has told me about the day Sage saved his life. His dad had been out of town for a business trip, so he spent the weekend with Sage's family. His dad came home early and had started drinking. When he didn't show up at school the next day Sage came to check on him and found him bloody, beaten, and barely alive. When his dad saw her, he pulled a gun and shot her, but she was a better shot and while the bullet hit her shoulder, her bullet hit him between the eyes.

He went to live with Sage's family that day, and not long later they adopted him. I met him right after that.

"Will you tell me what had been going on with Lee?"

"There isn't much to tell. I just got a vibe from him I didn't like. He would make some off the wall comments about me being his because I worked for him, or he would have me do things around the diner that weren't my job. He was always talking with my parents and commenting on things he shouldn't even have known about, like how I was having a hard time finding a teaching job and me spending time here with you. Jenna said she hates the way he looks at me."

"I can second that one, he gave me the creeps, and the way he looked at you like you were a piece of meat made me want to rip his eyeballs out."

"I never felt scared until today when he grabbed my arm. It's the only time he has touched me, I swear. I wouldn't have put up with that."

"Well I'm here and not leaving your side for the next ten days and I hope you will think seriously about coming out to the ranch with us. You can do as much virtual teaching as you want there, or maybe private tutoring. Mom knows the principal at the elementary school, we can see what openings there might be. Whatever you want, don't pick something because you feel you have to."

"You know that's why I went into education, right?"

"What do you mean?"

"I can be a teacher anywhere and that means I can leave my parents. That's why I went into education."

"Sunshine..." I hear him take a deep breath. "If you had a place away from your parents and could do anything, what would it be?"

"I don't know."

"Well think about it, I want an answer, okay?"

"Okay."

It's on my mind as I drift off to sleep.

· · · ● · ● · ● ● · · ·

I'm woken up the next morning to pounding on the front door. Since Mac's room is closest to the front of the house, it's easy to hear. I sit up at the same time he does, and we look at each other.

I sigh. "I'm willing to bet that's for me."

"Maybe, but you aren't answering it." He gets out of bed and heads to the door. I hang out at the end of the hallway where I can hear everything but can't be seen. I do see the guys make their way into the living room standing back but ready if Mac needs help.

I hear the front door open followed by Jenna's voice.

"Where is she?"

I sigh and step out, seeing both Jenna and Sky in the door and Mac blocking the way. As soon as he steps aside and they see me, they rush in and both hug me so tight I can't breathe.

"I heard what happened when I went in for my shift this morning and quit on the spot. I called Sky but she hadn't heard from you either so we both rushed here," Jenna explains.

"Now you need to tell us everything," Sky demands.

"I'll make coffee," Mac says as he heads into the kitchen. I pull Jenna and Sky out to the deck so as not to wake anyone else and we sit down in the lounge area that overlooks the lake. Sky wraps a blanket around us as we huddle together. I take a moment to take it all in then turn back to them. They are both watching me and when Jenna spots the bruise on my arm, she holds it up for Sky to see.

"Did Lee do this?"

"Yeah."

"Oh my gosh, Sarah, you have to press charges," Sky says.

"I agree." Mac comes out with a tray of coffee and cups. He makes all of us a cup and sits down next to me.

"I decided last night that I would. Mac's parents are going to help me. I guess Mac's dad called Beth last night, but I don't know what happened."

"I have a photo of Lee grabbing her arm." Mac pulls out his phone and shows the girls and they both gasp when they see it.

"So what's your plan?" Jenna asks.

"Well, today we are going to my parents' house and moving my stuff here. His mom's offered me a job cleaning and redecorating this place while I figure out my next move. I just know I need to get away from my parents, ASAP. I haven't even turned my phone back on after I walked out last night."

"Yeah, we know, I tried to call you first. I figured you were either at Sky's house or here since I knew you wouldn't go home." Jenna sips her coffee and watches me.

We talk a bit and Jenna gives Mac and Sky her opinion on Lee and some of the things he did. She recaps walking in and finding out that I'd quit. Apparently, Lee was there and pissed that he'd be a girl short this morning, but now he has no waitresses at all.

As we are talking, Riley comes out. "Pancakes are ready, come in and have some breakfast."

As we eat, everyone starts waking up and coming in for coffee and food. Mac and the guys make a game plan for heading to my parents' house.

"Well, we are coming to help," Jenna says.

"No," Mac says firmly.

"Excuse me?" Jenna almost yells.

Mac sighs and rubs his temples. "Listen, from what Sarah told me, her parents are going to side with Lee and this could cause problems. I don't like Sarah being there, but she has to be. I won't put anyone else in danger."

I see Sky getting ready to protest when Helen steps in.

"Sky, I need you and Jenna here to help me get things ready for Sarah to move in."

Sky and Jenna both look at me and I can see the battle in their eyes. They don't dare tell Mac's mom no, but they still don't like the idea of not going to help me either.

"Stay here and help. I promise we won't be long with the guys, we will have too much help, I don't have that much stuff."

Sky sighs. "Okay."

After breakfast we all head in to get ready, not really knowing what we are up against.

Chapter 9

Mac

"I'm not kidding, I don't have that much stuff, and half of it is still packed from when I moved back in. Bringing all three trucks is going to be overkill," Sarah tells me again.

"I want to make sure we get everything the first time and get out."

She sighs and puts her hand on my arm which causes me to lose my train of thought.

"Thank you for this."

"Don't you know by now I'd do anything for you, Sarah? All you ever need to do is ask."

"I know, but I don't know why."

I glance over at her before turning my eyes back to the road. "Ask me again after all this is over and I'll tell you, Sunshine."

"Okay," she whispers.

When we pull up to her parents' house there are a few cars in the driveway.

"Looks like they are both at home. Yay," she says sarcastically.

There is room for two trucks in the driveway and one on the side of the road, and we all follow Sarah up to the front door where she pauses.

"I feel like I should knock, this isn't home anymore."

I choose for her and ring the bell. A moment later Sarah's mom answers the door all put together perfectly without a hair out of place.

"Why are you ringing the doorbell, Sarah?" she huffs out. "And your friends need to go home, we need to talk to you."

"We aren't going anywhere, we are here to get her belongings," I say.

"No, you aren't. Sarah is not leaving."

"You can't keep me here, Mother, I'm a grown adult."

"Then maybe you should start acting like one." Her mom turns her gaze to me. "I suggest you leave, you're trespassing."

"Let's call the cops and tell them you aren't letting her get her essential items. I'm sure you'd love that report in the local paper." I level her with my gaze.

"Let them in and we can talk," I hear her dad call from inside the house.

I don't miss the look of pure anger on her mom's face and she steps aside letting us all in. One thing I love about my brothers is that they get it. Without having to ask them they are surrounding Sarah and protecting her.

"Where's your room?" Colt asks.

She points to the stairs. "Second door on the left."

Colt, Hunter, and Jason head up to start packing her stuff as her mom yells, "Get out here, you are not packing up a thing!" They ignore her as Blaze and I stand on either side of Sarah.

"Just where do you think you are moving to?" her mom asks.

"A friend's house."

"And what are you going to do for a job? You need the job at the diner." Her mother sneers.

"I already have another job lined up."

She looks shocked. "Doing what?"

"None of your business."

"It most certainly is!"

"No, it isn't. Once I leave here, I am done with you."

"Next stop is the police station so we can file charges on Lee," I say.

Her mother's eyes shoot to me. "You will do no such thing; this whole misunderstanding is ridiculous! You need to go to Beth and tell her you were upset and blew it all out of proportion."

I lightly take Sarah's arm and hold it up showing her mom the nasty purple bruise.

"This is out of proportion? You really think it's okay for men to bruise up your daughter like this?"

The guys come down just then with the first load to put in the trucks, but I don't miss the look of shock on her dad's face, and the look of indifference on her mom's.

"It's a misunderstanding, just talk to him. You're overreacting." Her mom waves her hand, dismissing it.

"How dare you. You are supposed to protect your daughter from sexual predators like that piece from trash, not tell her she's overreacting!" I yell.

"You know nothing. I bent over backward to get her that job and this is how she is going to repay him? He's been nothing but nice to her, trying to show her he cares, and now she is dragging him through the mud."

I take a deep breath and soften my tone. "Sunshine, go help the guys and make sure they get everything you want, please."

She looks at me, nods her head, and then heads upstairs with the guys. Blaze remains by my side, silent unless I need him.

"You know as well as I do that all she had to do was call up Beth and she would have had a job in a second," I say in a level voice as I take a step toward her mother.

To her credit she doesn't back up, she just raises her chin and watches me.

"What is really going on? Why are you so hell-bent on pushing your daughter into a situation where she has already been hurt and one that she is being eye-fucked daily by a man old enough to be her father?"

"You shouldn't make accusations you can't back up. It might end you in jail, Makya," her mother spews out, using my full name.

"I have photo evidence for everything including when he put his hands on her last night. Unlike you, I will protect her from that piece of shit and from you."

"Enough!" Her father stands up, finally saying something. "I think it's time for you to leave."

I nod. "As soon as Sarah has all her stuff, we will be gone."

Her father stares me down when Blaze speaks up. "Go help them, I'll stay here with them."

"We don't need a babysitter," her mom scoffs.

With one last look at her, I run up the stairs to help them.

"You guys almost done?"

"Yeah, we got all her clothes, just finishing up her desk and a few other things," Colt says.

"I told you I didn't have much." Sarah sighs as she loads up her stuff from the bathroom.

"How did it go?" Hunter asks.

I pull Sarah into my arms to calm me. "Not good. We need to hurry."

"Well, that's the last of the desk stuff," Colt says.

"Everything is out of the closet," Hunter adds.

"I got the stuff you wanted off the walls." Jason tapes up the last box.

"Anything else?" I ask her.

She looks around and then shakes her head. "No, that's it. The furniture is all theirs."

"Let's go. Her parents are up to something and I don't like it." I grab a box and we head downstairs, the guys loading the boxes in the trucks.

"You have anything left to say to them, Sunshine?" I whisper.

I watch her back go straight. "No, I'm not shocked by their response, I actually expected it."

"You walk out that door and you are cut off," her mom says.

"I got you," I tell her. "Anything you need."

"It's fine, I have been switching all my stuff over and you haven't paid any of my bills in months, but I guess you didn't notice. Don't call me, I have nothing left to say."

We start to walk out and her mom yells behind us, "You will be sorry, don't come crawling back to us when you fall flat on your ass."

"You have to be kidding me," Blaze mumbles under his breath.

"I'm just sorry I waited this long to walk away," Sarah yells back and we get in the truck and head home. The whole drive I just keep thinking about how proud I am of her and how strong she was.

Chapter 10

Sarah

As soon as we got to the house, the guys unloaded Sarah's stuff and Mac and his dad took me down to the police station to file a report on Lee. They took photos of my arm and my statement. Also Mac's statement, and a copy of the photo Mac took.

I guess the sheriff is friends with Beth and is going to call her and let her know. Apparently, there are whispers around town of Lee, but he can't do anything on whispers, only facts like I have given him.

We headed home but by the time I got there, Sky and Jenna have all my clothes unpacked in Mac's room and my boxes stored in the loft no one uses.

We sit down to eat a late lunch that Helen saved for us and fill her in on what happened at the police station.

"Sunshine, you look like you are about to be asleep on your feet." Mac furrows his brow in concern, "I know all this took a lot out of you. Why don't we go watch some TV in my room and you can take a nap?"

All I can do is nod because I do feel like I could fall asleep at any minute.

Once we are lying down all I can think about are the events so far today.

"You told me to ask you later about why you would do anything for me."

He sighs and looks at the ceiling almost like he was hoping I'd forget. "Besides my family, you are the most important person in the world to me. When you're happy, then I'm happy. Times like now when you aren't. Then neither am I."

I think about that and my mind only goes to one place.

"I'm sure your girlfriend must love that." I regret saying it the moment it is out of my mouth.

"For the love of God, Sarah." He sits up and looks at me. "What kind of man do you think I am that I would have a girlfriend back home and be lying in bed with you every night in my arms, holding your hand like I am? What kind of opinion do you have of me?"

"I just..." The words stick in my throat.

"Just what?" he asks gently. His eyes roam my face like he doesn't want to miss even the smallest detail.

"I guess I always thought you were a player."

He's quiet and studies me. "Why do you think that?" His voice is still soft and it's all I need to go on.

"You never talk about girls or dates. Sage and your sisters say you never bring anyone home or talk about anyone, but you act like this with me. Plus, have you seen you? I mean you are hot, I'm sure the girls back home are falling at your feet." I feel the heat climbing up my neck.

He shakes his head. "I don't date."

"So you are a player?"

"Can't be a player and be a virgin," he says and looks away from me.

What? Did I just hear him say that? No way did he just say he was a virgin? This hot, sexy cowboy who looks a lot like the werewolf guy from Twilight and that all the girls drool over is telling me he is a virgin?

"Mac?"

When he looks back at me there is a raw vulnerability in his eyes and a slight pink tint on his cheeks.

"I'm a virgin," he whispers, his eyes not quite meeting mine.

"Why?" My voice is shaking not sure why I blurted that out, but now I need to know.

"I'm not sure how to answer that." He cringes and looks away again.

"Is it because you don't want to have sex before you are married?"

"No. I've dated some, but the girls never held my attention, there were never really more than one or two dates. The tribe has tried to set me up with a few girls, but none of them held my attention. I refuse to lose it just to lose it. I want it to mean something." He shrugs. "What about you? You never mention any boyfriends."

"Because there haven't been any. I've been on a few dates, but I guess I'm like you. None of them have held my attention longer than a date or two. I also didn't want to lose it just for the sake of it."

He looks at me and his gaze is intense before he asks, "You telling me you are a virgin too, Sunshine?"

I nod because the way he is looking at me right now with the hunger in his eyes has my heart skip a beat and has me thinking wild thoughts like maybe he's been saving himself for me, just like I have been saving myself for him.

I know it can't possibly be true, but a girl can hope.

"I'm sorry for making assumptions about you, I was just putting together what I knew."

"You were adding two plus two and getting ten." He laughs. "Come lie back down."

I lie down and turn to face him, gathering my nerve before I lose it. "Want to hear something crazy?"

"Yes," he answers without hesitation.

"The reason my dates failed is because I compare every date to you. You would have opened the door and he didn't, you would have ordered the steak not the tofu burger, you would have gotten that joke, you wouldn't have said this or you would have said that. I just think you have spoiled me too much." I whisper the last part.

"I plan to keep on spoiling you. You should never settle, not ever. You are an amazing woman and the guy who is lucky enough to catch your attention should make you his whole world—build you up, protect you, and always let you know what you mean to them."

"Like you have?" I whisper.

"Exactly like I have," he growls, and before I can even register his movements, he launches for me and is pinning me to the bed, his lips on mine, kissing me. It's not a soft and gentle first kiss. It's a hard, punishing kiss, full of passion, need, and love.

He braces himself over me, putting just enough weight on me so I'm pinned to the bed. He has one hand on the side of my face cupping it and holding me so he can kiss me deeper.

"Sunshine," he whispers against my mouth, and the second I open my mouth to answer him his tongue is on mine stroking it and awakening every nerve in my body.

"Tell me you have been waiting for me like I've been waiting for you," he pleads against my mouth. "Tell me you compare every guy to me because you want it to be me on those dates, just like I wanted it to be you. Tell me so I don't have to stop kissing you because this kiss is better than any I have ever dreamed of." He rests his forehead against mine and I take a few deep breaths.

"Of course I've been waiting for you, who else is there? You consume my every thought, day and night. When I'm not talking to you,

I'm planning what the next conversation will be, the next time I get to see you."

"Thank fuck, cause if you said any other guy, I think I'd have lost my mind."

I give him a chaste kiss on the mouth. "I could lay here all day and kiss you but I'm on sensory overload and exhausted. I need to process."

He pulls me to his side.

"Get some rest. I will be here when you wake up."

My mind is racing. With everything going on with Lee and my parents, this is the last thing I expected, but I can't let this affect my goals. I don't want to make the choice to move to the ranch just for a chance with him. What if it didn't work out? I'd lose a friend, a job, and a boyfriend all in one swoop.

I have to put a stop to this, is the last thing on my mind as I drift off.

Chapter 11

Mac

The last few days there has been radio silence from Sarah's parents and Lee. A cop brought Lee in on assault charges and he has a court date. Sarah now has a restraining order on him, not that it means much. This family has seen before that it's just a piece of paper that won't stop someone.

We have spent the last few days just relaxing with my family. Lots of time at the lake watching Sarah in those skimpy bikinis she wears to torture me. She has spent a lot of time with my sisters and I know Sage has talked to her about moving to the ranch a few times answering her questions and promising if anything doesn't work out between us, she wouldn't lose her job and place to stay.

I hear Sage say I was the one in jeopardy of losing my room and being sent back to Mom and Dad's again, which made me laugh because I know she would do it just to keep Sarah around.

Tonight is the last night the family is here before they head out and then it's just Sarah and me. I'm excited but nervous too. Having the family here has kept us in check but without that buffer here, who knows. I like to think I will be able to be a gentleman, but no promises.

We are all sitting out on the deck with a fire going and the girls are making smores when Jason sits down next to me.

"So, has this week been everything you hoped to show Ella?" I ask him.

"Yeah, she loves it and already wants to know when we are coming back."

"This place is pretty magical." I have always felt that way, then again maybe it's just Sarah.

"Yeah, it is. So I guess her parents are talking about moving to Rock Springs."

Well, that's interesting. Not surprising because Royce, her brother, has a connection with Anna Mae, the hairstylist at Megan's shop. With two of their three kids here, there will be more grandbabies here, it just makes sense to move.

"What does she think of that?" I ask him.

"She's excited. She wants her family near, and after the church turned their back so easily on them over nothing really, they have no interest in staying there."

When Ella and Jason were dating, a guy from Ella's church tried to force her parents to get Ella's hand in marriage when she was almost engaged to Jason. He spread rumors and got them in trouble at church, and a lot of their friends turned their back on them. Even once it was exposed the guy was a fake and was wanted on rape and murder charges, their relationships never really bounced back.

I can't blame them. Who wants to be friends with someone who turns their back on you so easily without talking to you first? I think a move here would be good for them.

"Well you know there is room on the ranch until they get settled."

"Yeah, we told them that. They are talking about it and praying about it, so we will see."

Watching Jason with Ella, it's like they were always meant to be. They fit and have helped each other be a better version of themselves even though at the beginning you would have thought there was no way it would have worked out.

It reminds me of when Hunter and Megan met in school, you could just see the shift in them even though they fought their feelings for so long. Looking at them now, they just gravitate toward each other. One shifts and the other one follows. They laugh so much more now, and the town just loves it when Hunter's dad sits down in Megan's chair for a haircut.

I guess there was a misunderstanding between him and Megan a while back and the only way he could talk to her was to get his hair cut. Of course, the beauty shop is where the town gossips are so there was no hiding that conversation. He goes back each month now for a trim and is getting just as bad at the gossip as the ladies there.

"Colt, don't you dare!" Sage yells, and he sweeps her over his shoulder.

"What, you think you can get away with that and not get dunked in the lake, my wife?" He stalks down the step toward the lake.

I missed what she did, but this is still pretty funny.

"I'm sorry I didn't mean it!" She slaps his ass as he walks toward the lake. "Please, no, I'll do anything."

He stops but keeps her over his shoulder. "Anything?"

"Anything, Colt, just not the lake!"

I watch Colt spin and walk back up the stairs.

"Night, everyone," he says, and he heads inside toward their room. Everyone starts laughing and whistling.

Riley is giggling so hard she has tears in her eyes and Blaze places his hand on her belly.

"Calm down so you don't laugh the baby out!" This makes Riley laughs even harder.

"Oh god, Blaze, that isn't even a thing."

"Yes, it is! I read it online."

"You can't believe everything you read online," Sarah smiles.

The night goes on with lots of laughter, smores, and some good stories being passed around. We never do see Colt or Sage again until the next morning.

· · · · ● · ● ● · · ·

My family just left, and the house is eerily quiet now. Sage left me her truck, and she and Colt rode back with Mom and Dad. Sage said she was going to nap the whole way, having not slept much the night before. No one asked questions.

"Hey, Sunshine, want to walk with me? I want to check all the locks and windows make sure it's all secure since it will just be us here."

"Yeah, I love walking around this place, plus I can make a list of what needs to be cleaned and taken care of."

"If I know Mom, she had everyone strip their bed put the sheets in the laundry room, and remake the beds before they left."

As we enter Blaze's room, my theory proves true. We spend the next hour going from room to room checking on all the window and door locks. I'm sure Dad did this already since it's his routine before he leaves, but for my peace of mind and for my girl, I will make sure it is done again.

"Okay, now let me show you how to use the alarm, then we can check the kitchen and make a list to get it stocked up for you."

"I can go to the store and grab things as I need them."

"I'm sure you can, but I'm still stocking the kitchen for you." I shoot her my 'you aren't going to change my mind' look and she just shakes her head but has the hint of a smile on her face.

After our store run, we decide to lay out on the deck. She wants to read her book and I'm okay with just holding her in my arms, and that is how we spend the rest of the afternoon until I get up to make dinner.

"It's so weird without everyone else here, you really start to notice how big the place actually is." She sighs as we sit down to eat.

"Yeah, I've never been here alone, but some of my siblings have and they say the same thing. You going to be okay here alone?"

She shrugs and smiles at me. "I don't have much of a choice. Plus, my parents were never home and I got used to the house being empty. I'll make it work."

"You always have a choice. Have you thought more about coming back to Rock Springs with me?"

"I talked to Sage about it a bit, but it's such a huge move to make. Other than college I've never lived anywhere else and I always thought I'd just go where I get a job, no choice involved, but choosing to move somewhere new is scary."

"And you don't know the area because you have never been."

She nods.

"Well, why don't we head down there? It's only a couple of hours' drive. We can take the day to head down, spend a day and come back, or Sage can do a video call and show you the house and ranch and Megan can do one of the town on her lunch break one day."

She laughs. "I think I video call will do well. I just want to be able to see the place and picture myself there."

"I'll set it up."

After dinner, we watch TV and relax, and I hope there are many more days like this in the future. I just didn't know the uphill battle ahead of us.

Chapter 12

Sarah

I'm startled awake, but I don't know by what. The clock says it's 2:47 a.m. It has been just Mac and me at the house for three days now and it's been lots of lazy days, cuddling, kissing, and relaxing.

I know the pace of life at the ranch is different but if it was like this I wouldn't hesitate to say yes. I had problems falling asleep because I'm excited for the video call with Sage this morning and one with Megan this afternoon. That has to be what woke me up.

I look over at Mac and he is sound asleep facing me with his arm over my belly and it makes me feel safe. I have been falling asleep in his arms for over a week now. Could I really give that up in a few days when he heads home if I decide to stay here? Can I choose to move to Rock Springs just so I don't have to sleep alone? I still haven't made up my mind and I don't know what to do.

I'm running it all over in my head again when I hear a loud thump like something falling against the front door. My heart starts to race, and I shake Mac awake.

"Go back to sleep." He tries to swat my hand away.

"Mac, wake up," I say a bit panicked.

He sits straight up and looks at me. "What's wrong?"

"I heard a loud thump at the front door."

He jumps up and reaches into his dresser for a gun. I've never seen him with a gun in his hand before, but I remember the summer he learned how to use one, his dad was taking him to the shooting range every day. He would tell me he wanted to protect his family, but it was also necessary on the ranch with wolves, coyotes, and such.

I walk out into the hallway with him but stay behind the wall so I'm out of sight of the front door. Mac stops at the door and listens but from where I am, I don't hear anything. I hear him flip the switch for the outside light and open the door. I hold my breath but all I hear are his shuffling steps on the porch.

Minutes pass and he says nothing, and my nerves start to get the better of me. I go to peek around the wall to make sure he is okay, and I see him looking around the porch with his cell phone out. I stay silent but after a few more minutes he comes in and locks the door but leaves the light on.

"Anything?" I ask, taking in the worried look on his face.

"Someone was definitely out there."

My heart starts racing even more if that is possible and I don't realize I am shaking until I hear Mac.

"Shit, come here and sit down on the couch with me." He pulls me onto his lap and wraps a blanket around me.

"I was woken up by something, I don't know what, but I laid in bed and several minutes later I heard this loud thump like something falling against the door. That's when I woke you up."

He takes a deep breath. "Okay, I'm going to call the sheriff. There was someone out there. One of Mom's plants looks like it was fallen on, and there are footprints all over the porch, a man I'm guessing by the size."

I nod but make no move to get off his lap and he doesn't make a move to stand up as he calls the number the sheriff gave him when we filed my report. They remember him and say they are sending someone over right away and to keep the outside lights on and the doors locked. They have him stay on the phone and tell us when the deputy is there and that he is going to walk around the house. Mac gets up and turns on all the outside lights for him. They ask him some questions and the whole thing takes around half an hour with how big the house is.

When the deputy comes to the door, I'm at Mac's side, I want to hear what he has to say. Plus, this is a small town and news will travel fast, people will ask questions and want more information.

"Miss Sarah." Ben, a guy I went to school, with tips his hat at me.

"Ben, I didn't know you were a cop now!"

"Yes, ma'am, for the last three years. You living here?"

"For now. This is Mac, his family owns the place."

Ben looks at Mac and smiles. "Nice to meet you. Were you the one who called?"

"Yes."

"Okay, well like you told Wendy, the bush by the steps looks like someone fell on it and the footprints are all over the porch. It looks like it's the same dirt from the flower bed. There is a good one over to the side I will grab it for evidence before I leave. There are footprints all along the front of the house, but I don't see anything along the sides or the back." He looks down at his notes before he continues.

"Normally we'd say lock up and we will patrol the road a bit more, thinking it might be someone looking for an empty lake house to sleep in, but because of your report earlier this week we will attach this to it. It could be unrelated or not, there is no way to tell just yet. Make sure all your windows and doors are locked and the alarm is set even if you are in the house, just to be safe."

"We checked the doors and locks a few days ago," Mac says.

"I would do another round on them after this to make sure nothing is out of place and all. Like I said, I didn't see anything but it's better to be safe. Do you have any questions?"

"What are you doing with the footprint?"

"Well I have a spray I use, and then I take an imprint, kind of like your fingerprint. It's used as evidence. We can take the approximate height of a person, and if those shoes are used on another crime scene, then we can build a case."

I nod.

"Okay, I'm going to get this footprint for evidence, why don't you start checking the windows and doors."

Mac won't let me leave his side as we check all the windows again. All are still locked, and nothing looks out of place, and it's after 5:00 a.m. before we finally fall back into bed. Mac insists I try to sleep but my mind is racing as I lay there taking everything in.

· · · ● · ● · ● · ·

I guess at some point I was able to close my eyes because I wake up a few hours later to Mac kissing my neck.

"Wake up, sunshine, we can't sleep the day away."

"Mmmm, I feel like I could."

He laughs then looks me in the eye.

"I don't want to miss any time with you. But you have the video call with Sage in thirty minutes and I still need to feed you."

"Shoot." I jump up to get ready for the video call, and I'm ready with ten minutes to spare. As soon as I am in the kitchen, Mac is shoving a bagel.

"Eat up."

I'm just finishing when Sage calls.

"Hey, girl, Mac told us what happened last night. Hopefully, it's nothing. Are you okay?

"Yeah just tired, it messes with you when you are jolted awake at 2:00 a.m."

"Trust me, I know!" she says.

She spends the next hour showing me the house and what would be my little apartment downstairs. I try to act excited about it, but if I stay there then a whole floor is separating Mac and me. I've gotten used to sleeping in his arms at night. I'm not sure I want to give that up or if I will be able to sleep in the same house as him and not be in his arms.

She also shows me the room they want to set up for homeschooling the kids and says I can use it as an office for now. There is a pool, a huge front and back porch and while the house is massive, it looks cozy and lived in. She shows me some of the ranch around the house too and I try not to let on how much I love it. It feels like a home, even via video.

When I get off with Sage, I have less than twenty minutes before my video call with Megan.

The sheriff calls with an update for us. The shoe Ben dusted for is a size 12.5 men's and makes the man around 6'1 or 6'2. I swallow because that's about how tall I'd guess Lee is, but I have to be overreacting to think Lee was stumbling around the lake house at 2:00 a.m.

Megan's call takes my mind off it all and she shows me a little about her shop, but she does a video walk down the downtown area and points out the cafe, Jason's bar, the Dr's office, the veterinary practice where her husband works. She shows me the windows of some cute shops and even gets stopped to talk to a few people she introduces me to.

Everyone is nice and they all put their vote in for me moving there like if enough say yes then I can't say no. That just might be the case because Mac is watching me and smiles every time someone starts talking about the reason why I should move.

When I hang up with Megan, Mac pulls me on to his lap on the couch.

"So, what do you think?"

"Rock Springs reminds me a lot of Walker Lake, and I like that. The ranch seems great and the house is beautiful."

"That's all Sage, she's had a hand in almost every detail about it."

"It's still a huge step but I like knowing a bit more. I just need some more time."

"Take all the time you need, sunshine, I want you to be sure of your move and never once regret it. But I want you to do it for you. While there, you can do anything you want. Go back to school if you want, take any job you want. You will be surrounded by my family who will treat you like family and we will all support anything you want to do."

My heart warms at that. That kind of support is something I have never had. Mac has always been my biggest cheerleader and of course Sky and now Jenna as well. But to be surrounded by that with his family would be amazing.

Of course, moving means leaving Jenna. Sky has a job in Dallas, so in reality, I'd be moving a bit closer to her. I'd also be gaining Mac's whole family, all ten of them plus Mac, and I could be there for the birth of the kids from the start, and that would be amazing.

It makes all this so much harder. Ranch work isn't my thing and living on a ranch wasn't in my plan. Could I really move out there and make it work?

Chapter 13

Mac

I have Sarah in my lap and life is perfect. I see the wheels turning in her mind, and all I can do is hope and pray that her brain is cranking out good thoughts about moving to Rock Springs and the house and the town.

I nuzzle her neck, not being able to take my hands off her. The thought of our time together ending turns my stomach so I'm trying not to think about it and just think about today and the fact that she is in my arms.

I run my nose up her throat and she leans into me, wrapping her arms around my neck. I pull back and look in her eyes before leaning in to kiss her. It's a soft, sweet kiss not wanting to push things too far.

"Want to go swimming?" I ask her and watch her face light up. My girl loves the lake and being in the water. I love watching her in her bikinis, she has so many different ones I love seeing which one will show up.

When she walks out to the deck to meet me, she has a towel wrapped around her, so I take her hand and we head down to the dock. When she drops the towel, I think my eyes just pop out of my head. She is in a simple black bikini but one I haven't seen before, and it's skimpy. It basically covers her nipples and that is it, and as she turns to dive into the lake, I see the bottom is a thong. I'm instantly hard and I send up a silent prayer because in that moment I know she is trying to kill me.

I dive in after her and when I surface, she's laughing.

"Who are you wearing that bikini for?" I growl at her.

She winks with a big smile on her face as she circles me in the water. I let her make a complete circle before I grab her and pull her to me.

"Tell me, who did you buy that for?"

I watch a blush coat her cheeks. "Jenna bought it for me, but I've never worn it, until today."

She wraps her legs around me. We are in a spot where I can stand but it's a little too deep for her.

"You wore it for me, Sunshine?" I ask, my voice hoarse.

The blush deepens and she nods. I wrap my arms around her waist and look down at her full, perky breasts that are barely contained by the small scraps of fabric. I trail my hands down to cup her ass that is bare thanks to the thong bottoms. I kneed my fingers into the lush skin there and I know she has to feel how hard I am since she is pressed up against me. When she lets out a moan, I almost lose it.

She wraps her arms around my neck and wiggles against my cock and it's my turn to groan.

"Sunshine..." I whisper, but she doesn't stop. She tightens her legs around me and kisses me. It's a kiss full of need and I rub my hands up her sides to her breasts. I cup them and knead my fingers into them causing her to gasp and call out my name.

"Do you feel what you are doing to me? How hard you make me when you parade around in these scraps of material you call a bikini?" I trace the edges of the top triangles with my fingers then hook them and rip them to the side exposing her dark pink nipples. I spin around to press her to the leg of the dock, so her breasts are level with my mouth, and I take one of the stiff pink nipples in and suck on it hard until she cries out and thrusts her chest into my face.

"This what you wanted? To make me lose my mind?"

"Yes!" she gasps, and grabs hold of my hair, and pulls my mouth to her other breast and I give it the same attention sucking it into my mouth hard until she cries out again.

I bring her back down so I can look into eyes and she wraps her legs around my waist again.

"You aren't going to wear this swimsuit for anyone else are you, Sunshine?"

"Only you."

"Good, because all it would take is a nice strong wave hitting this top and letting guys get a look at these pink nipples and they would go crazy. They would see this sexy ass on display and think you were theirs to take and have their way with, but you aren't anyone else's, are you?"

I grip her ass and move her slowly over my cock.

"No," she whispers.

"That's right." I trail a hand around and rub her clit over the thin material of her swimsuit bottoms. "You aren't theirs. Whose are you, sunshine?" I need to hear her say it because her not being mine is about to push me over the edge.

When she doesn't answer, I take my hand away causing her to whimper. "Whose are you?"

"Yours, Mac."

"That's right. Only mine."

I pull her swimsuit aside and rub my thumb on her clit and her legs lock around my waist.

"Mac!"

"Yeah?"

"Oh god! Don't stop." She thrusts her hips at me.

"Couldn't stop if I tried." I rub faster and she hooks her fingers in my swim trunks then pushes them down.

"I want you, Mac."

I lean in and bite her bottom lip. "You have me. Always have, you just never knew it."

She moans again. "I want you inside of me."

My breath catches and every muscle freezes in place, causing her to let out a frustrated squeal and start grinding on me trying to get the friction she needs.

"That's not what this is about, I'll give you what you need but you don't have to do this."

"I want you, Mac. I've wanted you since that first summer we met." She places her hands on either side of my face, making me look at her. "Every dirty dream stars you. Every time I get myself off, it's to your face. This isn't a spur of the moment thing. It's always been you."

I take a deep breath trying to think over the sound of my heart racing like a freight train in my chest.

"I don't have a condom," I whisper.

"I've been on the pill for years."

"Why are you on the pill, Sunshine?"

"For my periods, they were really bad, it helps them." She shrugs.

I close my eyes again and rest my forehead on her. "Our first time and you are telling me I can go bare?"

"Yes, Mac, only you."

I almost lose it right then and there. My voice is lodged in my throat, all I can do is nod. I push her swimsuit to the side and rub my cock over her clit.

"I want you to come first, Sunshine, I need you nice and soft so this hurts as little as possible," I say looking into her eyes, and she nods.

I slide my cock over her clit, back and forth until she throws her head back and moans. I kiss her exposed neck and run my teeth over her earlobe and give it a light pull.

"You need to keep quiet, we don't need the neighbors wandering over and trying to get a glimpse of me ramming my cock into your virgin pussy and your tits bouncing everywhere, do we?"

My dirty talk sends her over the edge, and I take her mouth with mine to swallow her scream as she comes. I give a hard thrust and break the barrier of her virginity while she is riding the pleasure of her orgasm, and her cries turn to pain as she bites down on my lip to try and muffle the sounds. The pulsing of her pussy around my cock and the pain of her biting my lip causes me to come hard fast. I don't move inside her, just sit there until she lifts her head to look at me.

I'm still hard, so I watch her face for any twinge of pain and pull back slowly and thrust back inside of her. Seeing no pain, I do it again and her mouth drops open.

"Mac," she whispers. "I can feel you everywhere, it feels so good," she moans.

"Good, because I don't think I can stop. I should take you inside and make love to you on the bed, gently dragging it out for hours, but you sealed your fate the moment you walked out in that swimsuit," I growl as I thrust in and out of her.

"I don't want gentle, Mac." She gasps. "This is perfect. You, us, it's all I ever needed."

"God, Sunshine, you are my everything. I'm not going to be able to let you go now."

"I don't want you to," she moans.

"You. Are. Mine." I punctuate each word with a trust, slamming into her the last time.

"Yes," she screams as I feel her pussy start to pulse around me. I lean down and take one of her nipples into my mouth and bite it gently. Just enough to send her over the edge and take me along with her. She bites my neck to keep from yelling and the pain causes me to come even harder. The sensation over her clinging to me is something I can't describe. I've never felt anything like this in my life.

When she stops, she is limp against me and I need to catch my breath. Never once did I ever think I would lose my virginity to her in this very lake I saw her step out of all those years ago.

Chapter 14

Sarah

I am lying in bed trying to catch my breath after round three of sex with Mac, and I lost count of how many orgasms. After the lake, Mac dressed us again and carried me to the house and to the shower. He took his time and washed every inch of me playing with me and stopping after getting me right to the edge. Then I returned the favor. He took me up against the shower wall after that. It was sexy and quick and then he insisted on washing me down all over again.

He dried me off then dragged me to bed for a nap. I drifted off and he woke me up as he slid into me again and edging me several times before he let us both go, which brings us to now. As he pulls out of me, he pulls me into his arms.

"I need to feed you." He kisses my shoulder. "You stay here and relax I will be right back." I watch him climb out of bed and the muscles of his tan ass flex as he slips on a pair of sweatpants and heads to the kitchen.

Once he leaves the room the orgasm haze starts to clear, and I remember I still have to make a choice about moving to Rock Springs or staying here. I don't want that decision to be made based on a guy and mind-blowing sex. I mean, the sex is amazing, don't get me wrong but it's not what you should base life-changing choices on. Right?

I cover my face with my hands. What was I thinking going to the lake in that bikini? My head is already a mess trying to sort this out, did I think sex would make this choice any easier? I don't think I was thinking, just feeling. I need to call Jenna and Sky over and talk to them and get a non-lust-fogged opinion.

I grab my phone and pull up our group text.

Me: Hey, guys. I need some advice, are you free tonight?

Sky: I am!

Jenna: Me too!

Sky: We will be over in a few hours.

Jenna: Is this a wine talk or a tequila talk?

Me: Wine.

Sky: I'll bring stuff for smores, we can sit on the deck with some wine around the fire pit?

Me: Perfect I will kick Mac inside and tell him it's a girls' night.

Jenna: See you soon, girl!

Sky: Love you, girl!

I set my phone down just as Mac walks back into the room with two plates of food and bottles of water tucked under his arms.

"Everything okay?" He hands me a plate.

"Yeah, Sky and Jenna are going to come over for a girls' night, if that's okay?"

He sits down beside me on the bed and kisses my bare shoulder. "Of course, sunshine. This is your house now too, have them over whenever you want."

I take a bite of the BLT he made, thinking it over.

"Why do you call me sunshine?"

He chuckles. "Took you seven years to ask that, you know?"

"I always assumed it was because of my hair."

"Nope." He pops a chip in his mouth and looks like he is thinking.

"That day I saw you the first time, I was thinking about how lucky I was to have this family and I turned around and saw you walking out of the lake and it was like the sun was shining down and lighting up my life. It was showing me where I was meant to be. That summer, every time you were around, you would light everything up like a bright summer's day. When I said goodbye to you, everything was dark and dreary until I saw you again. That's why I call you sunshine."

I set my plate down and pull him in for a kiss. "You were the one good spot in my life, other than Sky, for so long. When I was having a bad day in college or didn't think I could do it anymore, one text from you was all I needed. After a phone call and I felt like I could climb Mount Everest."

He pushes some hair from my face and rubs his thumb along my cheekbone just looking into my eyes for a minute. I swear I see something on the tip of his tongue but instead he clears his throat.

"Eat up so you can get ready for your girls' night. I'm going to be in the office if you need me, catching up on emails and any paperwork they need help with at the ranch."

I can tell that's not what he was going to say, but I don't push it. The doorbell rings an hour later, and the girls pull me in for a huge hug when I answer the door. We head out to the deck.

"You girls need anything?" Mac peeks out.

"Yeah, for you to get out of here! No boys allowed!" Sky shoos him with her hands, making him laugh.

"Well, I'll be in the office if you need me." He closes the door with a big smile on his face.

Jenna pours the wine and they both sit down and look at me.

I sigh. "Mac and I had sex." I figure open with the big news get it out of the way.

"What?" Jenna squeals, all giddy.

"About time!" Sky says, laughing. "Your first time, right?"

I nod and they both go quiet.

"How was it?" Sky asks gently.

I think about it. How can I even begin to describe what happened between Mac and me at the lake?

"Mind blowing. Life changing."

They both giggle. "I knew that man would be good in bed." Sky sighs and I roll my eyes. She has said things like that before she went through a boy crazy stage. She has calmed down a bit since moving to Dallas.

"So tell us everything! Is he a good kisser? Did you come? How big is he?" Jenna rambles.

I glance toward the house. "Guys! That is between me and him!"

"Oh, he's small. It's okay, does he at least know how to use it?" Sky asks.

"He is not small, yes I came, and he's amazing, now that's it."

"Then why did you call us over here if you aren't going to give us all the details?" Sky asks.

"Because I need advice."

"Honey as long as he came, you are doing it right, don't worry." Jenna takes another sip of wine.

I roll my eyes and look up at the stars that are just coming out. "That's not it."

"Then what's up?" Jenna asks.

"I have a choice to make and I need to make sure it's not clouded by the sex haze I've been in. I need to tell you everything and get your opinions so I need you to be serious, this is the rest of my life. I can't make these choices based on some guy."

"Let's be honest, Sarah. Mac isn't just some guy."

"Sky!"

"Okay, okay!"

Their faces get serious and they both nod.

"Okay, let me start at the beginning, you might know some of this but let me get it all out." Again, they both nod.

So I start with the night at the diner when Lee grabbed my arm. I tell them about the talk Mac and I had in the parking lot and the two choices he gave me. I tell them about moving out of my parents' house and going to the police station and pressing charges. I tell them about the talks with Helen on the work needing to be done here and about my time alone with Mac for the last few days and how he was a virgin too. I tell them about the noise at the door this morning and about Sage's video house tour and the one from Megan around town. I tell them everything.

They nod, ask a few questions, but mostly listen to everything. When I'm done, they pour me my third glass of wine and hand me a bar of chocolate and both look deep in thought.

"So where is your head with all this?" Sky asks. "What are you thinking right now, before we tell you our opinions."

"I'm a little all over the place if I'm being honest. I'm scared to move out of Walker Lake. Getting a job, the choice is made for me where I'm moving to, I take the job and just move. But this feels different. Part of me wants to stay and do the work for Helen and put that money in savings and stay here to apply for jobs and see what happens. Part of me wants to go to Rock Springs once the work here is done." I take a sip of wine and think. "There is another part of me that doesn't want Mac to leave. I've been spending every night in his bed and the thought of spending one night away from him rips my heart out. I want to go with him when he leaves so I can avoid that feeling, but it's silly because I would be living in the downstairs apartment and still not in his bed."

"Maybe. I'm willing to bet if you are in the same house, he will either have you in his bed or be down in yours," Jenna says. "I've seen the way he looks at you. He's checked on you no less than five times from the door at the other end of the deck since you have been out here."

"Okay, all that aside, the move to Rock Springs is no different than if you got a job elsewhere and that is why you are moving. Take away Mac's family, the ranch, all of it, and just look at the job. Virtual teaching and tutoring kids on the ranch and Mac's nieces and nephews when they are old enough to start preschool? Do you want it?" Sky asks.

I think about it for a minute. It sounds better than any job I could have asked for elsewhere. Watching the kids grow up, not having new ones each year. I like the idea.

"It includes helping cook and clean around the ranch too."

Sky rolls her eyes. "It's a ranch, no matter what you went there for, its part of ranch life. Now answer my question, ignore the cooking and cleaning. Do you want the job?"

"Yes."

"Okay, now let's expand. It's in another small town and life on a ranch. Could you handle ranch life? Cooking and cleaning, I know you can do it, but are you okay with moving from one small town to another and living further out?" Sky continues.

"Yes, the small town was never the problem, it's always been about getting away from my parents."

Sky nods and Jenna takes over.

"Now, if you want the job and the location, what is holding you back exactly?"

"Mac. What if I move and we start this and it doesn't work out, and I not only lose a good friend, but also my boyfriend, my job, and my place to live?"

"Sarah, you think you will lose this job and a place to live? Do you think Mac would do that to you?" Sky rolls her eyes.

I sigh. "No and Sage has said the same, but it's still in the back of my head."

"Okay, then you have a backup plan. If something were to happen, you move in with me in Dallas until you get another job. No rent, just cook and clean. Done, now that argument is irrelevant. Next," Sky says.

I don't know what to say, so I sit there thinking.

"What if it does work out?" Jenna jumps in.

"I am almost scared to hope it could."

"Want to know what I think?" Sky asks, opening the second large bottle of wine for the night.

"I think you already know what you want to do. You are just too scared to admit it to yourself and you want us to validate your answer. So tell us what you want but are scared to do."

This is why I needed Sky here. She is blunt and knows me better than I know myself sometimes.

"I want to stay here, finish the work for Helen, then take the job in Rock Springs," I whisper. Scared because it's the first time I'm saying it out loud.

"I would tell you to just go when Mac goes, but I get you want that extra money as a safety net, so I support you. Plus, I want the extra time with you," Jenna adds.

"Rock Springs is not that far from here, it would make a great weekend trip," I say because I am going to miss her like crazy.

"I know, and I will be there often. Also, you can always stay with me, my parents would love to have you. I know you want to get out of Walker Lake, but it's an option too."

I lean in and hug her because what else can you say when you have amazing friends like them.

"So, decision made?" Sky asks.

I nod. "I will do the work here, then take the job in Rock Springs."

"When will you tell that sexy cowboy of yours the news?" Jenna asks.

I smile. "After you girls leave."

We spend the next hour talking town gossip and about Sky's life in Dallas. I really have missed nights like this and since I've been here with Mac, I've had more of them and I can only hope there are more to come.

Chapter 15

Sarah

I wake up and can't catch my breath, my nerves feel like they are on fire and I am on the verge of an orgasm. When I feel Mac's hand squeeze my hip again and I look down I see his head between my legs and feel his tongue on my clit, I almost come.

I reach down and dig my hands into his hair. He stops long enough to look up and smile at me.

"Good morning, Sunshine," he says, before his mouth is back on me driving me crazy. When he slides two fingers into me, the feeling is too much and my climax washes over me. I lay there like a limp rag doll with no energy to move as Mac comes to lie down beside me.

When the girls left last night, he carried me to bed and made love to me until we passed out. I never got the chance to tell him about my decision to take the job on the ranch. Now I barely have the energy to keep my eyes open.

Mac rolls me to face him and pulls me to his chest before he slides inside of me.

"My favorite way to wake up." I sigh.

"Mine too." His smile lights up his whole face. His thrusts are lazy and slow, and we both just enjoy the connection.

"Mmmm, you keep distracting me and I will never get to tell you my news."

"Tell me now, Sunshine." He keeps with his lazy thrusts.

"The girls and I were talking last night."

"Yeah, you guys seemed to have a lot of fun, I'm glad you have friends like that." His hand digs into my ass cheek and I lose all train of thought.

Mac chuckles. "What did you talk to them about?"

"You."

"Yeah, what about me?"

"All the dirty stuff," I say as I rub my chest against his.

"Mmmm, what else?" he starts kissing my neck.

"About the offer to move to Rock Springs," I whisper.

"What did they think?"

"That I should do it."

His thrusts pause so I start moving my hips, looking for the friction I need.

"What are you going to do, Sunshine?" he asks, his voice rough and almost like he is scared to know.

"Fuck me like you mean it, and I'll tell you."

He growls and flips me on to my back and slams into me so hard I have to reach up and put my hands on the headboard to stop my head from hitting it.

"Tell me," he growls.

"I'm going to stay here and work for your mom." I gasp.

He slams into me even harder and makes me cry out.

"Wrong answer, Sunshine."

He leans down my bites one of my already hard nipples.

"Mac! Once I'm done here, I'll move to the ranch!" I yell, right on the verge of a climax.

He stops thrusting all together and I let out a frustrated growl and try to move my hips, which is useless since he has them pinned down.

"You mean it?" He looks at me in awe.

I reach up and pull his head down to me.

"Yes, I mean it. Just a few weeks here so I can do the job for your mom and pad my savings," I whisper as I pull him down for a kiss and he starts thrusting into me again.

As he picks up the pace, I'm begging him not to stop again because I don't think I could take it.

"Not going to stop. You feel too good," he groans, right before strumming my clit and falling over the edge with me.

• • • • • • • • • •

"Why don't I just stay another week with you, and we can knock out everything on my mom's to-do list together?" Mac asks me for the third time in as many days.

"We've been over this already. You're needed at the ranch and I think some time apart will do us both good."

"I don't agree."

"I know you don't, you have expressed this to me at least twice a day now."

He grunts but keeps rocking us on the swing on the deck as we watch the sunset. He leaves to head back to the ranch tomorrow, and he isn't happy about leaving me here. I'm not happy for him to go but I think these few weeks apart will do us good.

"You will call me several times a day, right? Tell me everything about your day?"

"Of course. And you will take as many boxes of my stuff that will fit in your truck. I only need my clothes and computer, everything else can go with you."

"I'm going to unpack them too, might help if it feels like you are actually living at the ranch."

I can't help but smile. "Okay."

"Sage is excited that you agreed."

"I know, she keeps texting asking me what I need or want for the schoolroom she is setting up. She isn't even pregnant yet!"

"She's excited and loves to shop."

"I can tell. I guess she was in some school store in Dallas yesterday and she asked what theme I wanted the schoolroom in and sent me a picture of this huge aisle of themes. I told her to send me her top three choices and we settled on horses."

"It was always going to be horses, if you picked anything else, she'd have talked you into the horses and made you feel like it was your choice."

"Oh, I believe it. Poor Colt, I think she filled up his truck with school stuff for that room."

"She probably has him hanging it all up today too."

I laugh.

"I'm going to miss this," I say softly.

"What?"

"Just relaxing with you at the end of the day."

"We can do that at the ranch too. It can be an incentive to get your cute, sexy butt out to the ranch sooner." He kisses the top of my head.

· · · ● · ● ● · · ·

Watching Mac drive away was the hardest thing I've had to do in a long time. I cried and took a day to be sad and lazy, but then I started kicking things into high gear. The place is so big, it took me four days to clean the house from top to bottom and do the laundry. Also, Mac is calling constantly, saying he misses me and asking what I'm doing, or showing me things around the ranch.

He sent me a video of Sage working a horse that was abandoned and she took on to give it a new home. He shocked me when he said he talked to Sage and that it would be my horse when I got to the ranch and I needed to name it. Then we got into a fight over what to name it because he rejected my first three ideas and I now refuse to come up with any more.

He also video calls every night and we just talk about anything and everything. It doesn't compare to falling asleep in his arms, but it is the next best thing.

Today I am heading into town to get some of the items on Helen's list that need to be replaced. She wants new towels in the bathrooms, some new sheets for the beds, and a few cooking utensils that need to be replaced. She left me with her credit card, and I plan to make a day of it and drive the hour into Amarillo and hit the stores there.

It should be an easy shopping trip. Helen wants solid-colored towels and sheets, and simple black utensils to match what she already has. I talked to her yesterday and she said she had some stuff being delivered tomorrow for the house for me to put together. From what Helen told me it's some furniture to replace and some decor.

Sky went back to Dallas yesterday, but I called Jenna and she agreed to go shopping with me. On the way there we talk about what I have gotten done and what still needs to be done and she agrees to help me tomorrow as well.

Over lunch, she starts talking town gossip.

"Rumor has it, Beth is back in town, but I haven't seen her," Jenna says while finishing her burger.

"This is the first time I've left the house in five days, I know nothing and have seen no one."

"Well, the grapevine says that she is in town and she fired Lee because of what he did to you. She also found out he was fixing the books and stealing money from the diner making it look like the profit stayed the same instead of increasing. I guess she is pressing charges too."

"Wow, I had no idea."

"Me either, no one has seen Lee in town since he was fired, his neighbors say they see him getting mail and all, but he never leaves the house."

"Can't say I blame him. When the whole town is talking about you, the last thing you want to do is leave the house."

"Yeah, we have all been there at least once," Jenna agrees.

"It's all part of that Walker Lake small town charm." I laugh.

On the way home, we jam out to the radio, singing at the top of our lungs and just enjoying a girls' mini road trip.

Our high from the afternoon comes to an end when we pull up to the house and find the door wide open and one of the front windows broken.

"Oh shit, I'm glad I decided to come over for dinner," Jenna says. We aren't even out of the car and I can already tell it's bad.

"Sarah!" Jenna grabs my attention "I'll call the cops, you call Mac."

I nod.

"Hey, sunshine, what's going on?" he asks.

"Mac, someone broke into the house."

"What! Are you okay?"

"I'm fine. Jenna and I went shopping in Amarillo, we just got back the door is wide open and one of the front windows is broken. We are in the car and I can see the living room looks torn apart I know I set the alarm."

"Did you call the cops?"

"Jenna is on the phone with them now."

"Sarah, I'm on my way to you. I do not want you alone in that house until I get there, okay? Keep Jenna with you or go to her house. I'm going to pack a bag now and let everyone know what is going on. I'll text you when I'm on the road. If you head to Jenna's house, text me her address please."

"I will."

"Call me after you talk to the cops."

"I will, the sheriff and Ben just pulled in, I promise to call soon as I can."

Ben taps on the car window.

"Sarah, stay in the car with the door locked while we search the place and get photos okay?" Ben says.

I nod and watch him and the sheriff head into the house, guns in hand.

"They've been in there a long time," Jenna says, her eyes still on the front door.

"It's a big house," I say barely above a whisper, but I agree, it's been thirty minutes already.

It's another twenty minutes before they come out. "Well, there are footprints out back where it looks like they broke in. They look to be the same ones we found on your front porch the other night. Nothing big is missing, that we can tell, but the house has been destroyed... and your room... Have you talked to Mac or his family?" Ben asks.

"Yeah, Mac is on his way."

"Any way you try to get him on the phone? I'd like to talk to him."

I pull up his number and dial.

"Sunshine."

"Hey, Ben is here, he wants to talk to you." I hand the phone to Ben and he walks away from the car. I watch the sheriff walk out to his car and grab a camera and head in to start taking pictures.

"He's taking pictures, I wonder why?" Jenna murmurs.

When Ben comes back, he hands the phone to me and his face is serious, not even a tiny trace of friendly.

"Sarah." Mac's voice is firm.

"Yes?"

"I want you to go to Jenna's, the cops are going to do their job, but I don't want you to go in there."

"Mac, what's going on?"

"Can you do this for me, just until I get there? I'm getting in my truck now."

I take a deep breath and look over at Jenna. "He wants us to go to your house and let the cops do their thing."

I can see the look on Jenna's face, she knows, like I do, there is more to the story, but she nods.

"Okay, we're going there now. I'll text you her address."

Chapter 16

Mac

I get off the phone with Sarah and I have to take a few deep breaths.

"What did the cop say?" Jason asks. When I told everyone what was going on and that I was going back to Walker Lake, everyone said I shouldn't go alone.

Sage wanted to go and help out, it's her thing to be the protective one, but with Riley and Megan being pregnant we all put our foot down and said no, especially Colt. She is needed more with the girls. Hunter is needed for the animals, so Jason stepped up to come with me. He's driving since I'm on the phone, and because he won't break all the traffic laws getting there.

"It's the same footprint that was on the porch last week."

"Oh, shit."

"That's not even the worst part. I couldn't tell Sarah, I just wanted to make sure she didn't go inside."

He glances over at me and then back to the road.

"Whoever did it, tore the place up but nothing seems to be missing, other than her entire underwear drawer. There's cum all over our bed and 'she is mine' is written on the walls in blood red. They think it's just painted but they are still having it tested."

"Shit."

"Yeah. They now have this guy's DNA, but if he isn't in the system then they can't match him. They are dusting for prints and everything else now. They're going to lock down the house as a crime scene and get all the evidence collected."

Jason is quiet for a bit. "They have any idea who did it?"

"On the record, no, but Ben and I both had the same thought that it's Lee. Ben said that ever since we filed a report against him and Beth fired him, he hasn't been his normal self, but no one has seen him leave his house. Doesn't mean he hasn't, just that no one has seen him."

"So what's the game plan?"

"She comes home to the ranch and we don't leave unless she is with us."

"Is she going to want to go?"

I sigh. "She did before all this. Said she wanted to finish the stuff Mom asked her to do so she could save up some money. I will make up jobs, have her redecorate a cabin for Megan and Hunter or you and Ella if I have to, but I can't let her stay there."

"I know and we won't leave until she does, so let's just hope she agrees sooner rather than later."

"I can agree to that," I say and look out the window at the miles of Texas dirt passing us by as we head north. My thoughts race. If it's not Lee, who else could it be? Sarah is beautiful and I can't imagine anyone would be happy to lose her. She told me there hadn't been any other boyfriends, so I don't see a reason for any guy from college to stalk her back to Walker Lake.

My phone rings and I see it's dad, so I pick up.

"Any news, son?" he asks.

I relay everything I just told Jason to him and he sits on the other end of the phone quiet for a moment.

"My first thought is Lee as well. You need to ask her about anyone else that could do something like this, any signs of a stalker, anyone who kept asking her out at school or the diner."

"Dad, I haven't even told her about the bedroom. I asked her to go right to Jenna's so the police could do their jobs."

He's quiet again. I know he's thinking about his next words and waiting to see if I say anything else. He always taught us to sit back and let people talk themselves in a hole.

"You have to tell her, son, if nothing else she will see it when she tries to pack."

"All that is left in the house is clothes and her laptop. I will buy her new of everything, God only knows what this creep touched. I can't stand the thought of her wearing any of it, even after being washed."

"So tell her that. I'm willing to bet she will feel the same way, but she has to know even if she doesn't see it."

I watch more of the landscape go by because I know he's right.

"What do you want me to do about the house, Dad? From what I was told, it's trashed but nothing seems to be missing."

"Oh, son, I'm not worried about the house. Your mom is already on the phone with a company to go in and clean it and take inventory of what needs to be replaced or fixed. They are ready to go as soon as the sheriff gives the OK. If you could take photos to send to me in case we need them. You just worry about getting Sarah home to the ranch here."

Despite everything, when Dad suggests the ranch as Sarah's home, I can't help but smile. The rest of the drive flies by as I get Jenna's address and a call from the sheriff saying he wants to meet me there for a walk through. We decide to head there first.

As we pull in there are several cars in the drive, but I recognize Ben when I walk up to the house.

"Mac, good to see you again, wish it wasn't under these circumstances."

"Agreed." I shake his hand. "This is my brother Jason, he came to help out."

Ben introduces us to a few of the other deputies there.

"At first it looks like an ordinary burglary, but the TVs are still here. The electronics haven't even been touched and usually, they are the first to go when someone needs fast cash."

I nod and take in the overturned couch and pillows all over the floor. The coffee table is flipped, and a leg has broken off. That's just what I can see through the open front door.

"How did he get inside?" Jason asks.

"The glass door off the porch leading into what I believe is the master. Interestingly enough nothing in that room seems to have been touched."

He shows us photos from Mom and Dad's room, we see the glass door is shattered but everything else is in place. Bed perfectly made, not even a picture frame turned over.

"What about the rest of the bedrooms?"

"Drawers are gone through but not trashed, we think he was trying to find her stuff because not every room was touched. But her room was the worst by far."

He pulls up photos of our bedroom and my heart is racing. I have an idea of what I'm about to see based on the call earlier, but I don't know if I'm prepared. Jason puts his hand on my shoulder.

The room isn't just trashed, it's destroyed. Pillows ripped open, sheets torn, mattress slashed open, dresser drawers on the floor smashed with clothes in them. The only drawer left intact˙ is the one that held her panties; I was told they are all gone. There is a white substance on the bed that we have been told they believe to be cum, which will have his DNA in it so we can use it to bust him. The wall across from the bed has the writing. It does look like it's written in blood, saying, 'she is mine'.

"I would recommend having a professional come in to clean the house just to be on the safe side. If it were me, I'd trash everything in the rooms, clothes, bed, all of it, and buy new."

"That's my plan, the key is getting Sarah to agree," I whisper.

"Well, tell her to call me if she doesn't agree."

Jason's hand is on my shoulder again. "Let's get out of here and go get her, huh?"

I nod and take one last look at the photos before heading out to the car.

When we get to Jenna's, Sarah runs out the front door and meets me in the front yard, and all I can do is hold her tight. "Sunshine..." I croak out and try to think about what could have happened if she had been home.

She doesn't say anything, just holds me. I don't know how long passes, but eventually

Jenna comes up and says, "Let's get inside."

Walking into the house, I notice it looks to have been made by the same guy that built my parents' place, although it doesn't have the log cabin feel inside the house. We sit in the living room and Jenna's parents are there as well.

"Mom, Dad, this is Mac and his brother Jason."

"Nice to meet you, I'm Janet and this is my husband, Evan. Please sit down tell us what Ben and Robert said."

I must look confused because Jenna says, "Robert is the sheriff."

"Oh, sorry, I didn't catch his name. So, it's not good. I wish I didn't have to tell you, Sunshine, but I won't start us out by lying or holding things back, I want you to know that. The truth, always."

Her eyes soften and she nods, agreeing with me before I continue.

"The footprints match the ones that were on that porch the night before I left, they smashed a glass door in my parents' room and came in from the deck. Nothing was touched in the master, but in the kitchen everything was pulled from the cabinets, plates smashed. The living room was torn up, furniture flipped and broken, but all the electronics still in place. A few of my brothers' rooms, the dresser drawers were open but when they were found empty nothing else was touched until he got to our room."

"You sure it was a he?" she asks with wide eyes.

I nod and continue. "Our room is destroyed. Nothing really can be fixed..." I can't bring myself to say it, but thankfully Jason picks up and tells them what we saw in the police's photos and what Ben had told us, while I hold Sarah close. As I feel her start to tremble, I pull her on to my lap and hold her tight.

"Do the police have any leads?" Evan asks.

"Not officially," I say.

"Unofficially?"

"We think it might be Lee."

"I told Mom and Dad about what happened with him and why I quit." Jenna lets us know they are up to date.

"Sarah, we will need to replace all your clothes. Ben agrees, he said to call him if you don't believe me. I'd rather you not see that room and just let us take care of it. Was there anything that can't be replaced there?"

She shakes her head. "No, not that I can think of. My laptop?"

"It was smashed."

"It's going to take a few days to clean that place up, longer to repair things."

"Mom already lined someone up," Jason adds.

At that, Sarah sits up. "But I was supposed to clean it up!"

I rub her back. "Sunshine, they have to bring a professional team. It's a crime scene now," I say softly and her face instantly pales. "Besides, I can't let you stay there alone again. I want you to come back to Rock Springs with me, everyone agrees. They have a place set up and as soon as you give the girls your sizes, they are going shopping for new clothes for you, they love an excuse to buy clothes."

"Dad is out now replacing your laptop, it will be there and set up for you when you get to the ranch," Jason adds.

Sarah's eyes water. "I can't accept all that." She shakes her head.

"You can, I would have done all this even if we weren't together. I care about you. Let me do this and take care of you. Come home with me where I know you are safe."

She glances at Jenna and they seem to have a silent conversation with their eyes before she agrees.

"Well, Sarah can stay in Jenna's room, and Mac and Jason you can share the guest room. You are welcome to stay as long as you need." Jenna's mom says.

"Well, I think it might be best to get Sarah out of town so I can supervise the clean-up of the house?" Jenna offers.

"As much as we hate to see her go, I have to agree," Janet says.

"Me too, and I'm good to drive a few hours," Jason adds.

"That okay with you, Sunshine? Head out now put some miles between us and this town?"

She looks at Jenna again.

"Jenna and her family are welcome any time. You will see we have plenty of room for them to come and stay."

"Mmmm, you know I'm coming to see what they put in the water down there." Jenna eyes up Jason, making him laugh and shake his head.

"Okay, but you know I'm going to miss you like crazy!" Sarah stands up and hugs Jenna. I hate that she is leaving her friend, but I relax knowing that she will be safe. Jason is texting on his phone and I know he's letting everyone know.

"Wait!" Jenna says and rushes to her room. She emerges a few minutes later with a bag. "Here are some clothes you can wear until you get your own."

There are more hugs and tears before we are on the road. I'm driving her car while Jason drives the truck back and she has her head on my shoulder. I know it's been a long day and while I wish it had happened differently, I can't say I'm sorry she is finally heading home.

Chapter 17

Sarah

When we got to the ranch last night it was late and dark, so I didn't get to see much. Mac carried me up to his bed and we fell right asleep, with his arms wrapped tightly around me. I've never felt so safe, even after everything that happened in the last twenty-four hours. I must have slept hard because I woke up to Mac watching me sleep and the look on his face was amazing.

We showered together and ate breakfast, and now he is showing me around. We started with a tour and he showed every room downstairs but seemed to avoid a part of the house.

"What's over there?" I ask him, pointing toward the door we skipped.

"The housekeeper's apartment." His tone is flat.

"Oh, that's where I'm living! Let's go see it."

"No."

"Well, we can see it at the end." I shrug.

He grabs my hand softly, making sure I'm looking at him. "I mean no, you aren't living there."

"Don't be silly. Of course I am, Sage said so."

"No, you're staying with me. Your stuff is already been unpacked in my room."

"Mac, I can't stay with you."

"Fine, I'll move down here with you."

"Mac!"

"Sunshine, sleeping in this house without you in my arms is not an option, so up there, down here, or our own cabin, take your pick but we do it together."

Jenna and Sky were right, and it gives me a warm fuzzy feeling that he wants me in his arms every night. I can't help the smile that ghosts my lips.

"Stubborn man."

He smiles and kisses my cheek. "Come on, I want to show you the ranch."

He shows me the barn and explains Sage's horse training and how the ranch works. He shows me his parents' side of the ranch and just before we head in to say hello my phone rings; it's my parents.

"I can't avoid them forever." I sigh. Mac pulls me to a rocking chair on the back deck and sits me on his lap.

As I answer the phone, he wraps his arms around me. I put it on speaker for him to hear because I have nothing to hide.

"Where are you?" my mother's firm voice greets me.

"Home," I say.

"No, I am home, you are not here. So again, where are you?"

"Your house is not my home and hasn't been for a while. I am at my home and that is all you need to know. Anything else I can do for you?"

"Do you have a job? What are you doing for money? I told you we aren't paying your way anymore; I already canceled all your credit cards."

"Yes, I have a job, Mother. I haven't used a dime of your money in months I told you that already. I am an adult, I can take care of myself."

"Honey, Lee is worried about you." Mother's tone softens and Mac's grip on my waist tightens.

"Why are you even still talking to him? I filed charges against him, and you are still talking to him?"

"Honey, he is worried about that boy you are spending all that time with. He saw how he treated you at the diner. We saw how controlling he was when you were here at the house."

I see Mac open his mouth to speak but I put my finger to his lips and shake my head letting him know I got this.

He nods and sucks my finger into his mouth, lightly swirling his tongue around my finger while never breaking eye contact with me.

"Sarah, are you even listening to me?"

Mac smiles because he knows I wasn't. I clear my throat.

"Mac treats me like gold, he's sweet and protective. Lee is the one who put the bruise on me, remember? He's the one you need to be worried about."

"Oh, he said the bruise was already there, that's why he grabbed your arm to look at it." My mother dismisses me, and I'm not in the least surprised.

"That's bullshit and you know it!" I yell. I've never before raised my voice to her before, even though many times could have called for it.

"Watch your language with me, young lady. I am still your mother."

"Then maybe you should act like it!"

"I think Lee is right to worry about you spending time with this boy if this is how you are going to treat your own mother. I know you are with him. I suggest you pack up and head home if you know what's best for you."

"Is that a threat?"

"It's a statement that mothers know what is best. That boy isn't it."

I hear the click of the phone and pull it from my ear to see she hung up on me. I put my phone down and wrap my arms around Mac.

He gives me comfort and security without saying a word. When he pulls away, he frames my face with his hands and looks me in the eye.

"You okay, Sunshine?"

I nod and smile. "Show me the ranch, cowboy."

He smiles. "Tonight, you and me, we are going on a date. We did this all backward. I'm supposed to take you on dates before I seduce you into my bed."

I can't help but laugh.

• • • • • • • • • •

That night, before dinner, Mac tells me to go get dressed in jeans with something comfy and warm. I search through the clothes the girls bought me and I have to agree, there is something about the thrill of having new clothes. I put on dark blue jeans and a gray t-shirt with a blue and white plaid flannel over it. I leave it unbuttoned and put on the brown boots in the closet too.

When I come downstairs, I watch Mac's face light up.

"This is why I call you Sunshine. You are gorgeous without even trying."

I can't help but smile too. We head to his truck which looks to be already loaded up with a cooler and some pillows, and we head toward the back of the ranch.

"Everyone has their favorite spots on the ranch, spots they like to go to think or just love to be. We are going to mine." He reaches out to take my hand and I take in the ranch as we drive on.

About ten minutes and three gates later, he parks the truck next to a fence line.

"Wait here."

He pulls some stuff out of the back seat and I turn to watch him set up the bed of the truck with blankets, pillows, and a cooler. Then he comes to my door and helps me out and into the bed of the truck.

I look around and to the left is the fence line, but the view out the back of the truck is of an open field full of yellow wildflowers. There are no trees in sight, so it looks like the sky is touching the tops of the flowers as the sun starts to set. The colors from the sky start to complement the yellows perfectly.

"Mac, this place is beautiful."

He looks out over the field and smiles. "Many times, I'd come out here just to enjoy the quiet and let my mind wander." He pauses, smiling to himself. "It would always land on you, wondering if you were okay, what you were doing, and when the next time I'd get to see you would be."

I smile. "For me, there was this big tree behind the library on campus. It was the perfect spot to sit on the ground and use it as a backrest. It was far enough away from the main walkway that it was quiet, but close enough I didn't feel alone."

He nods and pulls out our dinner. We spend time just enjoying each other. He asks more about college and the people I hung out with and tells me more about his day to day tasks on the ranch and how much he loves it. He talks a bit about the reservation too and some of his friends out there.

When we are done eating, he sets the bed of the truck up so we can lie down and just cuddle. Looking up at the stars we try to find as many constellations as possible and see what shapes we can find hidden away.

Then he looks over at me. "I used to dream of days like this," he whispers. "The days when I'd have you on the ranch, finally in my arms just laughing and carefree. There were days I thought it was so close I could taste it, and there were days I never thought it would happen." There is a sadness in his voice, and I need to push it away.

I lean in and kiss him gently, just feeling his lips on mine and taking in how his scent overwhelms me so easily. Without breaking the kiss he shifts so we are both on our sides facing each other. His hand slides to the back of my neck and pulls me in to deepen the kiss while his thumb runs over my jawline tilting my head up just as our tongues meet.

"Sunshine..." He pulls back enough to rest his forehead on mine. "I love you, Sarah."

I gasp, shocked, not just at the confession of his feelings but because I so rarely hear him calling me Sarah unless he is introducing me to someone else.

"I love you too, Mac," I whisper back, and this time I can feel the smile on his lips when they meet mine as he rolls me to my back and cages me in. I love the feel of his muscled body against mine, even through all our clothes.

He kisses down my jaw to my neck just taking his time. I grind my hips against his causing him to moan.

"Don't start something you can't finish," he whispers and his hot breath against my ear only amps up my desire for him.

"I plan for both of us to finish." I smile and start reaching for his pants.

He grabs my hands and stretches them above my head. "Not here, this date isn't about sex it's about showing you how I plan to take care of you."

"Mac," I plead and grind my hips against his again.

"I got you, Sunshine." He kisses down my neck as he unbuttons my jeans and slides them off with my panties.

"Spread your legs." The timbre of his voice makes me even wetter as I do what he asks. Before I can think twice his mouth is on me and he is licking my clit like I'm the finest dessert and he hasn't eaten in weeks. I'm already on edge and it only takes a few strokes before my climax hits me, causing my back to arch up from the bed of the truck.

"Another," he growls and doesn't let up his pace, only this time he adds in two fingers and strokes me from the inside too.

"I can't," I whisper as I run my fingers through his hair.

"You can and you will," he doubles his efforts, hooking his fingers inside of me, causing me to fall over the edge with no warning and screaming his name.

I couldn't move if my life depended on it and I think he knows this because he helps me put my clothes back on before he pulls me over to cuddle with him and covers us with a blanket.

Right there, under the big Texas sky full of stars, in a field of wildflowers, I see the life I want... and I'm not scared to reach for it anymore.

Chapter 18

Mac

The last few days since our date in the field have been amazing. The girls took Sarah out to get her even more clothes, though I think they just wanted some girl time. The days just seem brighter with her here. I know it's corny, but it's true.

I wake up with her in my arms every morning. My favorite way to wake her up is by making her come. With my mouth, with my hand, with my cock, it doesn't matter as long as she wakes up with an orgasm, then I'm happy, and of course she is happy.

By the end of the day she is the one pushing me down on the bed and can't get my clothes off fast enough, and I love this side of her. She is confident and takes what she wants, it's so hot in and out of the bedroom.

She is getting along great with my family, but then again, she always has so that shouldn't surprise me. I'm thinking about our time in the shower this morning as I'm fixing this fence when my phone goes off.

It's Jenna and thinking it must be about the lake house, I pick up.

"Hey, how's the house?"

"Oh, it's fine we have a bigger problem and I want to make sure you know, and that Sarah doesn't hide it from you. I love her and I'm probably breaking the friend code right now."

"What's going on?"

She sighs. "Lee found out she left town with you and went crazy. He's been spending almost all his time at the bar. First, he was just mumbling things like she is mine, I'm going to get her back, they keep lying to her, but last night he was really drunk and standing outside by the courthouse, ranting and raving about how horrible you treat Sarah and how Sarah is his and you stole her away and he had a plan and an agreement. Ben arrested him and he spent a night in the drunk tank but was released this morning."

"What agreement?"

"No one knows but they all know you treat her like gold, and they all know about the report filed against Lee, it's a small town and all."

"What do you think?"

"Honestly, I don't know what to think, my theories are all over the place."

"Well, I want to hear them."

"So breaking the friend code," she mumbles.

"It's for her safety and you know I won't out you unless I have to."

"At one point, I thought Lee would take little things said at the diner and misconstrue them in his head to mean whatever he wanted."

"What else?" I can tell there is something else that she is holding back.

"Listen, I haven't voiced this to even Sarah, and I could be way off my rocker, but my gut is saying something is off about her parents and him. How much her parents tell him; how much they push them together. It's just... off."

"I've had the same thought but haven't said anything to Sarah either, but Blaze has said something to me. He was there when we moved her out and heard it all."

"Yeah I've never liked her parents, never felt comfortable around them, but I haven't known her as long as you and Sky have so I thought maybe it was just me."

"Nope, not you. I haven't liked them from day one. Then again, I was pretty sure they didn't like me just because I'm Native American."

"They don't like me because I'm a waitress."

"Yet they forced their daughter into the same job..."

"Yep."

I feel like we are missing something, but I can't put my finger on it.

"Okay, well keep your ear to the ground there for me and tell Sky to as well, that way if she hears anything, maybe we can figure this out."

"Will do."

"Hey, Jenna?"

"Yeah?"

"What do you think of getting together with Sky and doing a girls' night here on the ranch soon? Sarah has been saying she can't wait to show you guys around."

"I knew I liked you. I'll talk to Sky and see what her schedule allows."

"Okay, just let me know and I'll make it happen."

· · · · ● · ● · · ·

I spend the rest of the day with my mind a million miles away from the ranch until I head in for dinner. Sarah bounces over to me and leans up to give me a quick kiss.

"Sage spent the day showing me some of her favorite recipes, we made some freezer meals and I helped with dinner! I've never cooked for so many people before!"

Not only is there the ten of us—twelve if Mom and Dad join—but the ranch hands who don't have families come in and grab food too, so sometimes we cook for thirty people and some days don't have leftovers. It's a big change from what she's used to but judging by the smile on her face, I say she is adjusting just fine.

"Also, Jenna called me, and I need to talk to you, but it can wait until after dinner." I nod, thankful she is going to tell me and not keep it a secret.

No secrets.

Not anymore.

Not between us.

At dinner, talk circles mostly around 'Hell Week' coming up. It's what our family calls the seven to ten days we take to prepare the ranch for winter. I need to head down to the reservation and line up some of the guys to come help. With Riley and Megan pregnant they won't be doing much more than cooking to help out.

Ella and Sarah are new and still learning but they both want to help out a bit, but it will be hard on them not being used to it. It's working sun-up to sundown, no real breaks, as we do cattle checks and pull them into the pastures closer to the barns for winter, we get the last of the hay ready, winterize all the out buildings and vehicles, stock up on food and water, make sure we have enough wood for heating and cooking if needed. We rarely have a power outage, but we like to be prepared.

We all would move to one of the old family cabins we keep stocked with blankets and sleeping bags. It has a wood-burning stove for heat and a few fireplaces. Sage and Mom keep a nice set of cast iron pots there too. The bunkhouses are set up nicely, but anyone is welcome to join us there during that time. We keep it stocked with books, decks of cards, and board games so it ends up being great bonding time.

We also do any renovations needed to the buildings for safety. We don't normally get snow out here in the winter, but it can happen, so we like to be prepared just in case. What we do get is the rolling winds that even at thirty-six degrees can feel close to freezing.

After dinner, Sarah drags me upstairs with a pep in her step.

"Sunshine, I need a shower before you tear my clothes off tonight." I'm all sweaty and dirty from fixing the fence line.

She laughs. "That's fine, but I want to tell you about my call with Jenna as we shower."

I mentally groan, I'm not going to be able to concentrate with her in the shower with me, but there is no way I'm turning her down.

Once we get to our room, clothes start to come off in a trail to the bathroom. I start the hot water and Sarah tells me about her call with Jenna and how Lee is acting.

"Any idea what he means?" I ask her as I pull her into the shower with me.

"No, but Jenna says people in town think he means me, but other than that no one has any ideas."

I nod. "Well, I'm glad you are not there anymore."

"Me too." Her smile is one that I've come to know as her playtime smile. She is horny and ready for me and it's one of my favorite smiles on her.

She grabs the soap and lathers me up very slowly everywhere but my rock-hard cock that juts up between us.

"You missed a spot." My voice is hoarse.

"No I didn't, he just gets a special kind of cleaning."

"What kind of cleaning would that be?" I slowly push her against the wall, and she gasps when the cold tile hits her back.

"Would it be the kind it can only get inside you?"

"Yes," she moans.

I smile. "That's the best kind." My lips crash into hers and my hands go to her ass and dig in, lifting her up so she can wrap her legs around me as I slide into her. She does give my cock a good cleaning, twice, before we get out and head to bed.

Chapter 19

Sarah

Today Sage, Riley, and I are working on what they are calling the schoolroom. Right now, it's this big room at the back of the house that isn't being used. The guys moved out a bunch of boxes and stuff a few days ago. Now we have a big empty room and some of the things Sage bought a few weeks ago, a desk and a couch.

We are currently sitting on the couch looking at the room with Sage in the middle pulling up ideas on Pinterest for school rooms. We all agree on the horse, ranch theme, and that we want it to be fun. The room has floor to ceiling windows that overlook the barn on one side and the backyard on the other side. There are sheer white curtains on all the windows that still let in plenty of light.

We decide to go for one long table so the kids can all sit together instead of individual desks and colorful storage we plan to stock with crafts and paints for now as the kids are young this will be more of a playroom.

Sage wants to use one corner as my desk and office area now.

"If you don't decorate it and make it yours, I am going to do it for you! You will be doing some virtual teachings here and planning, so I want it to be comfortable for you."

"Sage this is better than any office I could have ever hoped to have! The view alone is better than anything I could put on the walls."

She sighs and Riley giggles. "You better do it, or she will do something like penises on the walls." Riley giggles.

"Yeah, explain that to your kids." I laugh.

Sage smiles. "We'd change it out before they could talk, but it would make for some interesting teaching videos!"

"Can you imagine!" I bust out laughing.

This is how Blaze, Colt, and Mac find us.

"Babe, don't laugh too hard or you will laugh that little girl right out!"

This causes Riley to laugh even harder. "Blaze, I keep telling you that is not how it works!"

We are all laughing now.

"You guys have a name yet?" I ask her.

"Of course, it's a girl so her name is going to be Lilly," Riley replies with a blinding smile.

I must have a confused look on my face because Blaze fills me in.

"Lilly is our friend now, but she was a stranger who saved Riley from her ex and brought her right here to Rock Springs, to me." Blaze looks at Riley with such love in his eyes.

We all talk a bit more before Blaze insists on getting Riley upstairs for a nap.

Colt takes her spot on the couch and pulls Sage into his lap.

"What plans did you come up with for in here, love?" Colt asks, kissing Sage's neck.

Before she can answer, Mac picks me up, takes my spot on the couch, and pulls me into his lap causing Sage and Colt to laugh.

Sage goes on to tell the guys about our plans for the room and Mac whispers in my ear while she is talking.

"We are going to help fill this room with babies, sunshine."

I turn to look at him and the heat in his eyes is intense. We haven't talked much about the future. I've thought about it being here on the ranch, but this is the first time Mac has mentioned anything like this.

"I see the confusion on your face," He continues to whisper "so let me make this clear. You are it for me. You will be my wife someday, hopefully soon. I will be putting as many babies in your belly as you let me, the more the better. I have been in love with you since the day you stepped out of the lake, it's you or no one, and now that I have you at the ranch I'm not letting you go."

His gaze is sure and unwavering. How can you argue with that?

I lean in and kiss him, softly, until the doorbell rings. I pull back and he has a huge smile on his face.

"That would be for you."

"Me?"

"Yes, Sunshine, you go get it."

Who could it possibly be? I make my way to the front door with Mac walking behind me. When I open the door two warm bodies attacking me in a huge hug, it takes me a minute to register it's Jenna and Sky.

"What are you two doing here?"

"Your man here arranged for us to spend the weekend on the ranch here with you. Something about a girls' night?"

"Oh yes, we kick the guys out and have a good old time." Sage comes up and hugs the girls too.

I look over at Mac. "You did this?"

"Yeah." The smile on his face is so big it reaches his eyes.

My heart is so full right now and over the last few weeks, nothing has ever felt more like home to me, almost like I'm meant to be here. These people feel like family and mean the world to me.

I slowly stalk toward Mac and put my hand to his chest pushing him backward ever so slightly. His eyes never leave mine and I whisper, "Everything you said on the couch just now? Yes to all of it."

I watch his whole body shudder and he rests his forehead on mine.

"I love you, Sunshine."

"I love you too, Mac."

"Aw, now shoo with you men, over to Mom and Dad's and send Mom over here to us!" Sage laughs.

We both laugh and he kisses my cheek. "See you tonight."

Mac and Colt head out and Sage grabs Jenna and Sky's bags.

"Come on, I'll put you two up in my favorite guest room. How do you feel about Christmas?"

"We love it!" they both say.

"Good, because this is my Christmas-all-year guest room that everyone thinks I'm crazy for, but I love it."

When Sage opens the door it's instantly Christmas, the walls are a dark tan color, white trim, and dark hardwood floors. The bed, dressers, and nightstands are all white wood. The sheets are a black and white buffalo check pattern with red throw pillows and a red throw blanket. There are small, white, frosted, matching Christmas trees with white twinkle lights on each nightstand and evergreen wreathes in the windows.

The room is magical and not overdone. With a few simple changes, it could be an everyday bedroom and that is what makes it so welcoming.

"Oh my gosh, I love this room!" Sky says.

"Well, you will have to share it with me because I'm not leaving." Jenna flops down on the bed.

"Deal!"

"Good thing that bed is big enough for, like, five people," I joke.

"So you can join us!" Sky bounces up and down.

"You better clear that with Mac, he hasn't spent a night away from her since she got here," Sage says, and it's followed by a bunch of aws and sighs.

Mac's mom shows up with dinner in hand, crockpot lasagna, and her famous brownies. "I even made some food and brownies to leave with the guys, I felt sorry for them."

"Do we want wine or margaritas for us non pregos?" Sage asks.

Margaritas, we agree.

"For us lone pregos, I have virgin strawberry daiquiris," Riley says to Megan.

Jenna snorts. "Isn't that ironic?" Which causes everyone to start laughing too.

Over dinner we talk about Sky's job, and what Jenna told me about Lee. I share a bit about my parents. Riley and Megan talk about their weird cravings and we all take guesses when Riley will give birth, I think we are all hoping for a Christmas baby.

After dinner we crank up some music and play a game of 'dirty would you rather' which has us laughing so hard at one point that Riley squeals.

"We have to stop. I'm going to pee myself!" We fall about laughing and at that moment the guys walk in.

"I can't breathe," I gasp between giggles.

It takes us a good ten minutes to calm down, and as we catch our breath I groan. "My abs hurt!"

"Mine too!" Sky says.

"You girls are too much. Come on, Sunshine, let's go to bed." Mac comes and takes my hand.

"Oh no, you can't have her tonight, she's staying with us!" Jenna jumps up followed by Sky.

"The hell she is," Mac growls.

"We are having a sleepover; you can do without her for one night."

"No." He pouts. "I've been without her for the last seven years. Now I have her and I know what it's like to have her in my arms, I won't sleep without her."

He sighs and looks at me. "That said, if you want to stay with them, I won't stop you. I will always make sure you have what you want. Always. But will you at least walk with me upstairs?"

"Of course, I have to go change anyway."

We all head over to get ready for bed and of course Mac manages to get his hands on me long enough for a quickie before I head in to see Jenna and Sky.

We stay up until after midnight just talking and laughing. I love my friends but as soon as they are asleep, I head back to Mac's room because I too can't sleep without him.

I crawl into bed and without a word, he wraps his arms around me and pulls me tight.

"I couldn't sleep without your either," I whisper.

"I hate to say good, but I do mean good, it means fewer nights apart."

"No more nights apart."

"I can agree to that."

Chapter 20

Mac

Today I'm heading down to the reservation to line up help for Hell Week on the ranch. We are in early October in North Texas, so the temperature is dropping to the seventies and it's the perfect time for this huge push on the ranch.

Mom and Dad's family has been close to the tribe on the reservation for generations. So when we have extra work on the ranch, we always offer it to them first.

After breakfast, Sarah walks with me to my truck. Jenna and Sky left yesterday, but while they were here Sarah had so much fun showing them around.

"Where are you going today?" she asks as I pick her up and swing her to sit on the side of the bed of my truck, which causes her to squeal.

"Out to the reservation." I step between her legs, wrap my arms around her waist, and watch her eyes light up.

"Can I come with you?" She wraps her arms around my neck.

"You want to go with me?"

"Yes! It's where you came from and a huge part of your culture and history, I want to see it and experience it." She leans down and gives me a soft, sweet kiss.

I have to look up at the sky and take a deep breath before I answer her.

"I'd love to show it to you, Sunshine." My voice is hoarse with my emotion. "Go get ready." I lift her down from the truck.

On our way to the reservation, she asks me so many questions and I answer each one. Things like what it was like growing up with the tribe, what memories I have, traditions, customs, and what it was like to go to school there and then switch to the school in town.

The tribe's offices are toward the middle of the reservation and she just soaks up the land and how much wildlife we see on the way.

"Where are we?" she asks as we pull up.

"This is basically the tribe headquarters, their office. While the chief doesn't have the duties he once did, he has an office here and it's run almost like a little business."

I hold the door open for her as we walk in. The main waiting area has so much of our history on the walls and is almost like a mini museum dedicated to our ancestors. She takes it all in while I peek my head into Mo's office and he smiles at me.

"Mac! Come in!"

"I have someone I want you to meet," I say, and wave Sarah over.

Mo stands and walks over to her and she tries to hide how unsure she is about greeting him.

"Who do we have here?" Mo asks.

"This is Sarah," I say and smile. Mo knows who Sarah is to me and Sarah realizes it too when she sees his whole face light up. He doesn't waste any time and wraps her in a huge hug.

"I've been telling you to bring her around for years, I'm so glad you finally listened! Sarah, I'm Chochmo, but you can call me Mo like everyone else."

"What does Chochmo mean?"

He laughs. "Mud Mound."

She smiles. "I feel like there is a story behind that name."

"There always is, but you have to get me pretty drunk before I tell you."

"Good luck, I don't even know the story behind it," I joke.

"Well, it's that time of year I'm guessing you are here because you have work at the ranch?"

"Yeah, Hell Week is coming up, we are looking to start in two weeks and could use ten guys this year. Riley and Megan are pregnant, so they won't be out in the fields and it's Sarah and Ella's first year, so we need to show them the ropes."

"I know some guys who could do with some work and are more than willing to help out. Same terms as last time?"

"Same terms."

He nods. "Deal." We shake hands and then he turns to Sarah.

"Come, let me tell you about our people."

Mo spends the next hour going over all the photos in the waiting room and telling Sarah everything and answering her questions.

On the way home, she has a huge smile on her face. "I love it there, and Mo is an amazing storyteller."

"That's his job, to keep the stories and the history alive."

"What are the terms for the guys coming to work on the ranch?"

"They stay on the ranch, get the room and meals included, $100 a day cash, and the tribe gets three cows."

"Three cows?" she says, almost like she misheard me.

I laugh. "Yes, it's a tradition between my family and the tribe going back generations. When Blaze's several-times great grandparents settled on the very land the ranch is on now it was different than anything from out east and you had to tend it differently to get the grass to grow to take care of the cattle. They worked the first year with the tribe and in return, they gave them a slaughtered cow of meat. At the time that cow fed the tribe well, we were much smaller then."

"So you keep with tradition?"

"Yes, any time we have extra work we offer it to the tribe first and we pay for it, but for Hell Week the payment includes cows. It's not necessary anymore but neither side is willing to break tradition."

"I like it, it's deep-rooted. I hope you never break it."

Chapter 21

Sarah

The day before Hell Week, ten guys from the reservation show up. Five stay at the bunkhouse on this side of the property and five head to Blaze's side to get settled in. I thought I would be ready for the early days if I just went to bed early, but I was so wrong. No matter how much you tell yourself you are ready to get up and be ready to work by first light, you really aren't.

Day one is cattle day. Hunter is on the ranch helping with shots and health checks. Half the guys are out moving cows toward the barn and the other half are working the cows already there. Seeing so many cowboys in one place does something to a girl.

I take several photos and send them to Jenna and Sky, and they are so mad I didn't tell them sooner so they could have made plans to be there for the week.

My mom has been calling me every day, and every day I send her to voice mail—you would think she would get the hint by now. She always leaves the same message:

"Sarah, it's your mother, call me back today."

Pass. Delete.

With the guys in the fields during the day, they don't stop for lunch, so Ella, Helen, and I bring lunch out to them along with water.

Day two has been checking up the other animals on the ranch and starting on the hay.

Day three is Mac working a tractor in the back field. I take the truck out when I take him his lunch. I park the truck at the end of the row he is working and wait for him to meet me there. I take my phone out and snap a few photos. We are in a field near the one that we had our first date on the ranch in and it's just him and me. He's on the tractor that is, of course, that famous John Deere green, but instead of one with a closed cab, he's in an open air one.

There have been many country songs written about a man up on a tractor and in this moment in time, I can see why. I can vouch that there is something to it.

As he reaches me, he shuts the tractor down and climbs off. Today he is just in Wranglers and a t-shirt but he still looks every bit the cowboy with his hat and boots.

"Hey, Sunshine."

"Hey, I brought lunch and water."

He wraps his arm around my waist and pulls me close for a quick kiss.

"Perfect timing, I need a break." He sits down on the grass with his back to the big tractor tire and then pulls me down to his lap.

"Why don't you use the tractor with the closed cab?"

"It's such a nice day out I wanted to enjoy it. There are so few days in Texas that we can use this old tractor."

We have lunch talking about the work going on at the ranch. My phone rings again, and this time Mac sees it's my mom before I hit decline.

"What does she want?"

"I don't know, I have no desire to talk to her and she won't leave a voice mail. Eventually, my voice mail will get full and she will take a hint."

"Want to ride a few passes with me?"

I can't help but smile. Do I want to ride up on the tractor with this sexy hunk of Texan cowboy? Yes, please!

I nod and smile. He climbs up and then helps me up and on to his lap. He explains how it works and once we get going, he lets me steer. Being my first time on a tractor I don't get it very steady but it's not too bad that he can't fix it in the next pass.

When we get back to the truck, he parks the tractor and I stand and turn to face him and straddle his lap. He tucks his hands into the back pockets of my shorts and looks at me.

"This isn't fair, Sunshine, you're going to leave me all hot and bothered until after dinner."

"I was planning on taking care of you." I grind on his hard cock that I can feel through his jeans. He groans and leans in to kiss me. One hand trails around to the front of my shorts and slides up the leg to the front of my panties.

"Are you wet for me?"

"Yes, watching you on this tractor is so damn hot."

I feel his smile against my lips. "We better make it quick before someone comes out here looking for you and gets a glimpse of what is mine."

I stand up and remove my shorts.

"Leave the panties on," he says. Heat flashes in his eyes when he sees my black thong. He unzips his jeans and pushes them down enough to free his cock and pulls me back to his lap, then he moves my thong to the side, and I slide down him, easing him into me in one stoke, causing us both to moan.

"Oh, Sunshine, you feel so good, so tight." I brace myself with my hands on his shoulders and start moving up and down him while his hands on my hips help set the pace.

"I feel so full, Mac."

"Good, I want you heading back to the house full of my come so all those ranch hands know your mine. I see how they look at you."

My whole body shudders at his words. I fall forward burying my head in his neck to soften my moans.

"Then you come out here with lunch and a ride on the tractor has you all hot and needing my cock. Anytime you need it, Sunshine, it's yours. Only yours. I will always give you what you need."

That is enough to throw me over the edge and I scream out his name and he follows right behind me.

Chapter 22

Mac

Hell Week lasted eight days. Not the shortest one we've had but not the longest either. To have it all done and be ready for the first cold snap is a weight off everyone's back. Now we are just in cleaning mode. The girls have gotten together and deep cleaned Mom and Dad's house and are now doing our place. The guys and the ranch hands have been working on cleaning and organizing the barns and all the outbuildings.

Next week Ella, Sage, and my mom plan to do a bunch of canning from stuff in the garden, so we are still pretty busy.

I am working on paperwork in the barn office when my phone rings, it's Megan.

"Mac, we might have a problem."

"What's wrong?" She instantly has my full attention.

"People are talking about a guy in town asking around for Sarah."

Since Megan owns the beauty shop, she hears all the town gossip in real-time. The ladies like to gather there to talk daily so she always lets us know what is going on.

"What guy?"

"No one knows his name; he's just saying he needs to talk to her and it's important. No one will tell him where she is, most don't even know who she is."

"What does he look like?"

"I asked and the descriptions vary."

She goes on to describe what sounds like a tall guy, a little older than me.

"Oh, well, I will ask her if she knows anyone like that."

I wrap up what I am doing and go in search of Sarah. I find her and the girls cleaning guest rooms and talking about redecorating them.

"Sunshine, take a walk with me?"

We head for a walk down the driveway with no place in mind.

"Megan called me and told me some guy is in town asking for you."

"Who is it?"

"No one knows he won't give a name but says it's important."

I give her the description Megan gave me.

"It almost sounds like Nate from school. We had a lot of the same classes, so we studied together a lot."

I tense up. Some guy is looking for my girl and they used to spend a lot of time together.

Sarah notices me get tense and laughs. "We spent a lot of time together studying, with his boyfriend."

I relax and can't help but laugh at myself.

"I haven't heard from Nate in a while so I really have no idea what he would want or how he found out I was here. If he would go anywhere to look for me, it would be Walker Lake and if he was in town Jenna would have told me. But he has my number, so why not just call?"

"Well, Rock Springs protects our own. I don't think anyone will send him here, but we can have him stop by and see Megan and he can call you that way?"

"Sounds good."

I see we are near the ranch church without really having a plan to walk this way.

"Have you seen the ranch church?"

"No. Is that it?" I can hear the excitement in her voice.

"Yeah, Riley got married in the barn by the house, but Sage, Megan, and Ella were married here, so were Mom and Dad."

I take her inside the small white church. It holds so much history.

"Wow, this is so beautiful, Mac! I bet the weddings were amazing. I hate that I missed them because of school."

"You should ask the girls to see the photos."

She looks at me. "Do you want to get married here?"

"I want us to get married here someday." I don't break eye contact with her.

She smiles and looks around again. "I think I'd like that too."

· · · · ● · ● · · ·

The next week is a weird one. No one comes to talk to Megan about contacting Sarah but a few days later Jason calls me.

"Hey, man, there are whispers at the bar of a guy here in town asking for Sarah."

"Megan said the same thing earlier this week. Anyone get his name?"

"Nope. People have said that they ask and he just walks away. From the sound of it, he's asked everyone."

"Have you seen this guy?"

"Nope. If he has been avoiding asking any of us, I doubt he will come in here."

"Well, if I was looking for someone that no one wanted to tell me, I'd show up at the bar get someone drunk enough you never know what might come out."

"Very true. I'll be on the lookout."

"Okay, I'm thinking we should keep Sarah at the ranch for the time being until we know who it is. She thinks it might be her friend Nate from school, based on the description, but he has her number, so why not just call? If this guy won't give out his name, he can't be good news. There is a possibility the descriptions are off and it could be Lee."

"I agree, brother. Do what you can to keep her there but try not to scare her until we know more."

Things are quiet for a few days then Mike, one of the ranch hands, comes up to me. He and a few guys were checking on the outlying cabins making sure they are stocked and ready if anyone gets stranded out there.

"Mac, one of the cabins looks like someone has been living in it. It's pretty trashed and out of food."

I get Colt, Sage, and Blaze, and Mike takes us out to the cabin. It's the closest one to the main house only about a twenty-minute drive down the trail.

We get in and sure enough, the smell alone is a good sign someone has been here. The trash on the floor is our next clue.

"I haven't touched anything, thought you guys would want to see it," Mike says.

We split up and check every corner of the place. The canned food has all been eaten and there are beer cans everywhere.

"I think it's a guy, based on the ripped-up shirt I found in the bathroom," Blaze says.

"So do you think they plan on coming back?" Mike asks

"I don't know but being the place is out of food, I'd say no. Still let's get this place cleaned up and set a few motion cameras around the cabin see what we catch," I reply, looking around.

"Sounds good. I don't want anyone coming out here alone, and bring a gun when you do. More than likely could be a drifter, we've had them before, but better safe than sorry," Blaze states.

"I agree, Blaze, we should also have everyone stay away from this area for a few days, they can head to your side and the cabins there," Sage adds.

It takes us a few hours to get the place clean and the motion cameras up.

The next day, things in the barn are just off. It's like everything had been gone through overnight and is just slightly out of place. None of the ranch hands claim to have done it and it just seems to throw everyone off as we try to get things done.

The following day I get into the office and it's clear the office has been gone through. Everything is just enough out of place and all the drawers are open. No one goes in here but family, so I send a text to everyone asking them to meet me there.

"What's up, Mac?" Mom asks as she and dad show up, they are the last ones to get there.

"The office has been gone through, see for yourself. Pair it with the barn having been gone through yesterday and someone living in the cabin, I don't think it's a drifter."

"Me either." Sage sighs.

"This is too close to the house for comfort," Blaze says, and I'm sure he's thinking of Riley being pregnant.

"The guys have been watching the cameras we set up, and nothing but animals have triggered them. Maybe he moved to another cabin because that one was out of food?" Colt suggests.

I rub my hand down my face. "I think it wouldn't hurt to check, in pairs, with a gun," I stress.

"I'll stay with the girls at the house, Mom and Dad can stay with me," Sage adds, and Mom and Dad agree.

"Megs, maybe call in and not head to the shop today. I will stay home with you, you need some rest too," Hunter suggests.

"Sounds good to me, as long as you stay too. Riley and I can work on baby plans and do some online shopping."

"I was thinking about a movie day on the couch." Riley laughs.

"Ella and Sarah were working on redecorating my room, so I'm sure they will stay busy all day." I smile.

We pair up and head off to check the cabins, but something in my gut isn't sitting right with all this.

I'm paired with Mike who has been around the ranch for a while. "Something's on your mind.," he says.

"Something doesn't seem right with all this. It's not a drifter, and I think whoever was in the cabin was the one who went through the barn and the office." I try to work through it in my head

"I agree."

"So, what do they want?"

"I heard someone was asking about your girl in town, could this have to do with that?"

"Seems too coincidental to not be associated, right?"

"Exactly."

"Who could be after your girl?"

Lee's face jumps to my mind. Could it be him? And I left her at the house. I know Sage can protect her, but I can't help but think maybe being away from her would be what someone wanted.

"Let's make this quick, if it is Lee then separating us might have been his goal."

We get our horses to a dead run to find the cabin empty and untouched. We race back to the ranch only to find my worst nightmare.

Chapter 23

Sarah

Ella and I have been redecorating Mac's room all morning. We aren't changing the tribal feel he has, just adding more storage for my stuff. His room already feels like home, he was ok with me changing it all out. I laughed because my favorite part about the room is that it feels like him when I walk in.

I was a little bit on edge today with someone asking about me in town and now with the news of a stranger on the ranch, even though I feel safe here with Sage and her parents.

So when Mac suggested Ella help me with the room I jumped at the chance to get my mind off everything going on. Even though this whole mess sucks, I can't help but smile because I was included in the family group text this morning. To know they already consider me family is a feeling I can't pin down. I've never been part of a family like this and I was scared to dream I ever would.

I've been watching the texts start coming in that the cabins are empty and haven't been touched.

A text from Jason comes in just as there is a loud crash just outside the house.

"What was that?" Ella asks as we both race to the window. Mac's window looks out over the front of the house and we don't see anything but the massive green lawn, so we head downstairs.

Mac's dad is standing by the stairs, gun in hand facing the kitchen door. Instantly I'm on high alert and my heart start racing.

"Sage and Hunter went outside to see what it was," he says when he sees us.

"We couldn't see anything from Mac's window," I tell him.

"It came from by the barn on the side of the house," he says. We are all quiet trying to hear what we can. Megan, Riley, and Helen are in the kitchen making lunch but even they can't keep their eyes off the window. I'm guessing by their faces that they don't see anything.

A moment later we hear a gunshot, and time slows down as everyone hits the floor. My heart races trying to justify why a gun would have gone off. We are on a ranch, maybe it was a coyote in the barn or a rattlesnake. I've seen them shoot rattlesnakes in the movies.

Everyone looks around and seeing we are all ok we slowly get back to our feet. I'm trembling and can't open my mouth to ask even the most basic questions. Turns out I don't have to.

The side door bursts open and along with the flood of daylight from the door there stands Lee. It doesn't look like Lee as I know him from the diner. That Lee is always put together in nice pants and a button-down shirt, his face is always cleanly shaved and not a hair out of place.

This Lee in front of me hasn't shaved in days, it doesn't look like he has showered either, his hair is all greasy and messed up, his eyes are bloodshot, and his clothes are torn, stained, and dirty. His gaze flies around the room and then lands on me. He sneers and goes to take a step toward me but instantly, Mac's dad is in front of me with his gun, pointed at Lee and blocking his path.

"Stay right there, Lee, and tell me why you are on my land."

"I'm here for her." He nods at me. He seems unfazed there is a gun pointed at him

"She's not going anywhere."

"The hell she isn't, she is mine, I paid for her." He takes another step toward me.

The room spins and I have to grip on the banister to keep from falling over. I take a deep breath and force myself to focus when I hear even more commotion. I look up to see Mac rushing in the door behind Lee and tackling him to the ground, slamming him face first on the wood floor, his head to the side as he struggles to break free. Moments later, Hunter and Mike, the ranch hand are helping to hold him down. Sage comes running in and puts herself between Lee and the girls in the kitchen.

"Explain yourself," Mac growls.

"Sarah is mine, I paid for her," Lee yells, and Mac slams his head on the tile.

"Paid who?"

"Her parents." Everyone gasps or whispers, and it's then I see Sage has her phone out and is recording all this.

Mac looks up at me with confusion and rage.

"What do you mean you paid her parents for her?"

"She moved back in with them after school and they were about to lose their house, so I made them a deal. I'd pay them monthly for her. She was to work at the diner with me get to know me, they stopped her from getting any job offer so that she stayed in town."

"Where were you getting the money? That house isn't cheap, and I don't see a diner manager making money like that."

"Where do you think? Beth had me doing the books. I raised profits at the diner and took them for myself."

Helen gasps then and her hand flies to her mouth.

"Everything was going great until you showed up." Lee snarls and tries to fight the guys.

"Was it you in the lake house in her room?"

"Of course it was, she was supposed to go home to her parents, not here with you. Her parents were able to stop her from getting those stupid teacher jobs. It was a full-time task too, she was getting a few offers a day."

"What?" I manage to get out. I thought I didn't have enough experience, or maybe hadn't taken the right classes and that's why I wasn't getting any job offers.

"Your parents put tracking software on your computer they were able to retract most of your applications and deny the offers that did come in before you ever saw them."

I feel nauseous. I didn't get along with my parents but I never once thought they were capable of something like this.

"Was it also you in the cabin and going through the barn and my office."

"Of course, know your enemies and keep them close and all."

At this point, my knees do give out, but Ella, who hasn't left my side, helps ease me down to sit on the stairs.

"When you ran off with this guy, I demanded my money back from your parents and figured I'd come to get you myself. Nothing is going to stop me." He struggles again managing to throw off Mike from one of his legs but gaining no leverage with Hunter and Mac, who are sitting on his back and restraining his hands.

I hear sirens in the distance but with so much information surfacing it's hard to be relieved by it.

"That's where you are wrong." Sage smiles. "I got all this on video and that will be the cops I called. We don't take kindly to trespassers here in Texas, in fact, the last one is dead so consider yourself lucky." I had completely forgotten Sage had her phone out with my brain trying to process everything going on in my head.

Lee starts flailing all over the place trying to get loose as Blaze walks in with the sheriff. Hunter and Mike stand up as the sheriff goes to cuff him and Mac holds him down. Lee tries to make a break and lunge for me but he only makes it a few feet before the sheriff slams him back to the ground.

Once Lee is in the back of the cop car, Mac pulls me into his arms.

"Sarah, you ok? He didn't touch you, right?"

"No, he didn't get close, thanks to you."

When the sheriff walks back up, Sage starts giving her story and the video over to him. Then the whole story starts to come together.

The noise we all heard was Lee's attempt at a distraction by slamming some barn doors. When Sage and Hunter ran out to see what was going on, they ran into Lee who didn't get his gun out quite fast enough.

Mac starts in on how he rode up and saw Sage and Hunter struggling with Lee to get the gun away. It fired and Lee dropped it and ran into the house. No one was hit with the bullet, thankfully.

That point is where Sage's video picks up. I need to remember to thank her later for that.

Mac has hold of me in his arms through it all. By the time he is done talking to the sheriff, there is a paramedic on the scene who is checking everyone over, but I notice he is spending a lot more time with Riley. I assume because she is pregnant but when I see Blaze's face, I know that's not it. I rush to her side.

"What's wrong?"

"She is having some contractions and cramping, they are going to take her in to monitor the baby," Blaze says.

I watch them load Riley on the stretcher and she smiles.

"I'm sure they are just overreacting."

"I'd rather overreact and make sure you are ok." Blaze follows them out the door.

"Well, I have what I need. I know you guys are going to follow them to the hospital. I know where to find you," the sheriff says.

After that, it's a mad dash to make sure Mike has a handle on the ranch hands before we all file out to the trucks and head to the hospital.

· · · · ● · ● · · ·

We have been at the hospital for a few hours now and since there are so many of us, we wait in the family waiting room on the labor and delivery floor while Blaze, Sage, and Mac's mom are back with Riley.

Sage comes out and everyone jumps up all at once asking how Riley and the baby are.

Sage gives a tired smile. "She's good. There was some bleeding and contractions, so the doctor gave her a steroid shot to develop the baby's lungs faster in case she has to deliver early, but the contractions and bleeding have stopped. She has to stay on bed rest for the next several weeks. Strict bed rest, feet always up unless she is going to the bathroom or her doctor appointments, which will be more frequent now. The doctor told Blaze to get an at home Doppler to monitor the baby's heart rate, so he already ordered it on Amazon with overnight shipping."

"This was brought on from the event with Lee, right?" Megan asks.

"Yes, the doctor thinks it was the stress from the event at the house, but he is running some tests too, just to rule other things out. She has to stay overnight because her blood pressure was high when she came in and they want to watch it over the next twenty-four hours and make sure it doesn't spike again."

I don't hear what anyone else says at that point all I can think of is that Riley is in the hospital because of me. She could have lost her baby because of me because I came here to the ranch when I knew I shouldn't have. I should have stayed in Walker Lake and figured it out like I had planned. But in walks sexy Mac and my brain loses all rational thought.

Riley doesn't need this kind of stress of everything going on with Lee and now my parents. I haven't even confronted them or told them that I know everything that has happened. I still need to call Jenna and Sky, so they hear all this from me. I'm sure Ben needs to know about Lee as well.

Then there is Megan, who is also pregnant, what if the stress gets to her too? She is still in her first trimester; it would be so easy for her to miscarry and there would be nothing the doctors could do. I can't do that to them.

I feel a hand around my waist pulling me from my thoughts.

"Hey, Sunshine, let's get Megan and Hunter home. Megan needs to relax."

I nod and follow them out. The whole time my mind is racing with my 'to do' list.

When we get home, Mac goes to head in.

"Hey, I need to call Jenna and Sky. I'm going to go sit out front. I'll be in when I'm done, okay?"

Mac studies my face for a minute then he nods and places a soft kiss on my forehead.

"See you inside, Sunshine."

I slowly walk around to the front porch and stare up at the large column at the front of the house which is two stories tall. Everything really is bigger in Texas, including my problems. Life seemed so much easier when I was out of state at school.

I sigh and call Sky first and she listens quietly when I explain everything starting with someone asking about me in town to the events the last few days, leading up to Lee showing up and Riley in the hospital. When I'm done, she sits quiet for a moment.

"Oh, Sarah, what do you need? I can be there in two hours."

"Oh no, they don't need more people here. Riley is in the hospital tonight, I guess it's just a holding pattern until tomorrow to see what the doctor says and how she is overnight."

"Any more on your parents?"

"No, I'm going to call Jenna and give her a head's up, then call Ben. I'm sure the sheriff here will call and fill them in, but I want to see what they have to say as well.

Afterwards, I recap it all to Jenna who put her parents on speakerphone to hear it all and they are all at loss for words.

I sigh. "Jenna, I need a favor."

Chapter 24

Mac

When Sarah came back in from talking to Jenna last night, she seemed a little off, but once we climbed into bed she seemed back to her normal self. That's why I'm struggling with the letter I just found on her pillow this morning.

Mac,

I love you. I do. I have never felt more loved or at home than on the ranch. You showed me what it was like to be truly loved and I will never forget that.

I love your family like they are my own. That's why I won't let my drama bring them any more harm. Riley could have lost her baby because of me and with Megan pregnant, I won't take that chance. I will keep them, and you, safe.

You will find a girl who won't come with so much drama and so much baggage and your family will love her, and she will fit right in. I just don't think I'm that girl.

Take care of them and know you are truly blessed.

Love

Sarah

The hell I will, and the hell she isn't. How could she think what happened with Riley was her fault? Where did she go? She wouldn't have gone back to her parent's house, right? No. She wouldn't.

I've tried to call her no less than eight times in the last ten minutes, and I have worked myself into a small panic when there is a knock on my door. Colt peeks his head in and takes one look at me and his face goes stone cold.

"What's wrong?"

I can't even talk so I hand him the note and watch him read it.

"She really thinks this is her fault?"

I nod. "We got home yesterday she said she had to call Jenna and Sky and let them know what happened with Lee. She came in and was acting a bit off, but by the time we went to bed, she seemed fine. I woke up to that on my pillow. I've tried to call her, but she won't pick up."

Just then, my phone rings, and I lunge for it where I had tossed it on the bed. It's the sheriff, and my heart races with all the worst possible cases flashing through my mind.

She was so upset she crashed.

Lee made bail and got to her.

Her parents got to her.

I'm on the verge of a panic attack and I'm thankful Colt is here. He answers the phone on speaker.

"Sheriff, it's Colt, Mac is here."

"Mac, I wanted to let you know that Lee isn't posting bail. He will stand trial here for the attack on the ranch and then be transferred to Walker Lake to stand trial for the break in, money laundering of the diner, and the transaction he admitted to with Sarah's parents. The DNA came back from the bed at the break in up at Walker Lake, and it is a match for Lee. The substance on the wall did test as paint though. Due to the nature of the crime, he will not be offered bail, you and your girl can rest easy."

Rest easy? I wish. I don't know where she is if she is okay, or what her parents are doing.

"Her parents," I manage to croak out.

"What he means is, what is going to happen to Sarah's parents?" Colt clarifies for me.

"We have a warrant to the local judge to verify his story via bank transfers. Both Lee and her parents. If it proves true, we will issue a warrant for their arrest. Walker Lake has also taken her laptop in evidence, so they have their tech guy on it to see if there is indeed software on it. I was told to recommend getting her a new phone as well in case any software was installed on her device."

My heart lunges to my throat. I should have thought of that, and now I can't do it; I can't make sure she is safe. Who knows what her parents have on her phone, and now she is vulnerable and without me.

As soon as Colt hangs up with the sheriff, I grab my phone and text her. I know her phone isn't off because every time I called it would ring instead of going straight to voicemail, so I just pray she reads it.

Me: I just talked to the sheriff; you need to get a new phone ASAP. They think your parents might have bugged your phone. Lee won't make bail, but they haven't brought your parents in yet.

I wait, and nothing. Another five minutes, and nothing. My heart is racing and I'm getting dizzy. I sit on the edge of my bed, so does Colt.

Me: Sunshine, please answer and let me know you are okay and that you will get a new phone today. Have the store call me, I will pay for it. Please.

A few minutes later I get a text but not the one I was hoping for.

Sky: I will make sure she gets a new phone.

"Sky texted me. Does that mean she's there?"

"Maybe. Listen, take it from someone who had their girl run away. She needs time, but not too much time. Come run some cattle with me today, keep busy. Then tomorrow, if it's still radio silent, you go after her and fight, okay?"

I take a deep breath. I know Colt still kicks himself for not going after Sage all those years ago, and I won't make that mistake. I plan to fight for her, and for us, but I'm going to do it right and that means it's time to go talk to my dad.

"I'll meet up with you after lunch, got a few things to get in order if I'm going to fight for her."

Colt studies my face then nods.

After breakfast, I head over to Mom and Dad's house and find them both on the back porch where they normally enjoy their morning coffee. It looks like they are trying to get back to their normal routine and I don't blame them.

"Hey, baby, let me get you a cup of coffee. Did you eat already?" My mom asks, already halfway in the house. I know what I say won't matter, she will bring coffee and food back with her, so I just wait.

My dad sets his phone down and looks me over. I know he can tell something is wrong, but he doesn't dare get me to talk before Mom comes back out.

Mom sets my coffee on the wicker coffee table and hands me a plate of sticky buns.

Sarah would love these.

That thought sets me on edge, and I couldn't eat if I tried.

"Makya, I don't know what's wrong, but you will eat," she scolds.

"Sarah left."

"What do you mean left?"

I pull her note out of my pocket and let them both read it. Then I tell them about the call from the sheriff earlier.

Mom shoves the plate of food back at me while I'm talking, and as soon as I'm done, I take a few bites to appease her. Then I tell them about me texting her and the text I got from Sky.

"Do you have a plan to get that girl back? Because if you don't, I'm not going to be very happy." Mom puts on her fake mad face that would normally get a smile out of me but all I can manage is a slight tilt of my lips.

"I have part of a plan. She is it for me, I will go after her tomorrow; I'm going to give her today to calm down. I also came here to get my mom's ring, it's time."

I watch Mom's eyes water. When my dad died there was no will, so everything went to my sister who turned eighteen just a few weeks after he died. There wasn't much to divide up, some photos, and a box of my mom's stuff. One of the things I got was my grandmother's wedding and engagement ring. My mom wore on her right hand from the day they died until the day she died.

The rings have been kept in the safe here at the house since the day I joined the family. I knew early on either I'd use them to propose to Sarah or I'd give it to one of my nieces or nephews, there was no other option.

Dad nods and heads inside and Mom points a look between the plate with the half-eaten sticky bun and me. I sigh and finish up the food on my plate before Dad gets back outside and it puts a smile on my mom's face.

My dad hands me the box that holds the ring and I take a deep breath. I haven't seen it in seven years. As I open the box and see the ring that I always remember on my mom's hand, all the times I've pictured it on Sarah's fill my head, and my vision goes blurry.

"I don't know what I will do if she says no," I get out, barely above a whisper.

Mom comes and sits next to me. "Baby, I've watched you two from that first day and I know she is it for you. I had a feeling back then, but when she went off to college, I knew. Just be honest with her, make it big. Show her you know her better than she knows herself and don't come home until she says yes. We can cover things here, it's slowing down. Go get your girl."

With one of her famous python-tight mom hugs, she sends me off with another sticky bun and a few ideas to woo my girl.

Chapter 25

Mac

It's been twenty-four hours of radio silence from Sarah. Sky did text me last night telling me Sarah had got a new phone but kept the same number. I thanked her and didn't push her. I am now pacing the kitchen waiting for 9:00 a.m. to hit so I can leave. I don't want to get into Dallas too early and have to deal with the before-coffee Sarah.

"For the love of Dixie, just go, Mac!" Sage walks into the kitchen and rolls her eyes at me, so I change the subject.

"How's Riley?"

"Good, she comes home today, and Blaze has their room all set up with everything she could possibly need. He got her an emergency leave from school which she wasn't happy about, but he promised as soon as the baby was born and she was ready, she could go back. He also set up a rotation, so she isn't alone during the day."

"I hope to be home soon, and you will have two more people to put on that rotation to help out. Maybe more if I know Jenna and Sky."

Sage hugs me before I head out to my truck which I had packed up earlier this morning since I couldn't sleep last night. I point my truck towards Dallas and crank up the radio for the hour drive ahead of me.

· · • • • • • • · ·

After hitting a bit of traffic I'm pulling into Sky's place an hour and a half later, and my nerves are now hitting me. I know I'm not backing down and I have several back-up plans in place, but I'm hoping this will be easy.

I step up on to the porch and ring the bell. I don't hear any movement inside, but Sky's car is in the driveway, so I ring the bell again, this time I hear a muffled voice.

"Hold your damn horses, will ya. Good Lord almighty." The door opens and Sky leans on the door frame looking like she just woke up.

She sighs. "What are you doing here, Mac?"

"I came to talk to Sarah." What does she think I'm doing here? My heart races as I wait for Sarah to appear behind Sky.

Sky sighs. "She isn't here."

"When will she be back?" She must have gone out for a coffee run then, and if I know my girl her comfort food, donuts.

"Listen, come in and let me get some more coffee, she and I were up late talking." She opens the door and lets me in. While she gets some coffee, I take in her small place, but I don't see a sign of Sarah.

I sit on the couch and wait for Sky to talk. I try to be patient, but my nerves are getting the best of me and I can't seem to sit still.

"I was up late talking to her on the phone. She isn't here and she hasn't been here. I did make sure she got a new phone, I was with you on that one. I was on the phone with her when your texts came in, she told me. I also knew she wouldn't text you back and you were worried so I broke friend code texting you, again."

I run my hand over my face and my stomach sinks. She isn't here, I was so sure she would have run to Sky, she was her back up plan after all.

"I don't suppose you will tell me where she is?"

She laughs. "Mac, Mac, Mac. You just went in the wrong direction is all." She looks over the rim of her coffee cup and doesn't say another word.

It clicks a minute later. "She went back to Walker Lake."

"Yep." She smirks at me but studies my every move.

I close my eyes and take a deep breath. "Please tell me she didn't go to her parents."

"God no. You think I would have let her?"

I let out a sigh of relief. "She's with Jenna."

She shrugs but the kind of a smile on her lips tells me I'm right.

"Sky, she is it for me. That day I met you two, it changed my life." I pull my mom's ring out of my pocket and show it to her. "I plan to marry her, and I don't care how much drama follows her or how much baggage she thinks she has. We are in this together and have been since the day she walked out of that lake in that red bikini. Her dad doesn't mean a damn thing to her, hell you have been more of a parent to her than her own family, so I'm here to ask your blessing to marry her. I will spoil her and take care of her. I will give you tons of nieces and nephews and your own room at the ranch so you can visit as often as you want. I will plan monthly girls' nights, and keep up with the trips to Walker Lake. I will help her find the perfect job that she will love, not that she feels she has to take. I promise not a day will go by where she doesn't know how much she is loved and wanted, not just by me but by my whole family."

I take a deep breath and watch Sky stand up and walk over to the window with her back to me. She is quiet for so long that I worry about her response.

"Mac, I've always been your biggest cheerleader on the Sarah and Mac team, and I know you will treat her right, that has never been a doubt in my head. You need to tell her all that and more. She needs to know that you aren't leaving her, you aren't backing down and she can depend on you even when she is pushing you away. You have my blessing, under one condition."

"Anything."

She laughs. "Be careful, you never know what I'm asking for."

I look her in the eye confident in my next words. "There is not a thing you could ask for that I'd say no to if it meant I had your blessing to marry your best friend. I know I'm going to need you in my corner for this."

She doesn't break eye contact with me for what feels like minutes but in reality, is only a few seconds before she lets out a huge smile.

"Good. This girl deserves the world and I know you will give it to her but if you are going to pop the question, you need to do it right. It needs to be huge and mind-blowingly awesome."

"Blowingly is not a word."

"It is now, and is that what you really want to harp on about right now? Tell me about your plans. You do have plans, right? Please, for the love of sweet tea, tell me you came here with plans."

I smile. "I have plans, only they were based here in Dallas because I thought she was here with you. I need a few to change things up. While I do so, will you please call Jenna and check on Sarah? I promise not to make a single noise, I just need to know she is okay. Her parents are still out there, and... I just need to know she is okay."

Sky nods. "Not a word or I will help Sarah run from you, got it?" I nod, and then she mumbles, "This is breaking so many friend codes."

Sky gives me another stern look as she pulls out her phone and the next thing I hear is the ring tone on loud speaker. My heart starts racing and time stands still when I hear Sarah's voice.

"Hey, Sky."

"Hey, how are you doing this morning?"

Sarah sighs. "I'm good. I have to run my old cell phone down to the station today, they want to have their tech guy look at it, and Ben promised me an update on what's going on so I was just getting ready to walk out the door."

"Okay, be careful and text or call and let me know what Ben says."

She agrees and they hang up. I hate that I didn't get to talk to her, but knowing she is okay is everything. Now it's time to switch up my plans.

Chapter 26

Sarah

I get off the phone with Sky and close my eyes. I need to get out of bed and get moving, but finding the motivation to do so just isn't there. Jenna laid in bed with me last night with Sky on video chat, and we talked. I told them everything that had happened from the time they left the ranch.

They listened and ask questions then shared a look they didn't think I saw. They told me they are here for me and that I need time to think. In friend terms, that means they think I made the wrong choice.

It took me forever to get to sleep last night. Every time I closed my eyes, I saw Mac. I know I took the coward's way out and left in the middle of the night, but I couldn't face him either. He'd have been able to talk me out of it. It killed me a little more every time I didn't answer his calls or his texts. So when Sky said she'd text him about the phone, I agreed. I didn't want him to worry.

I drag myself out of bed and get dressed. Downstairs, Jenna's mom greets me. They were so welcoming when I showed up yesterday.

"Sarah! I made French toast for breakfast. Evan is already in his office and the boys are at work. Jenna is around here somewhere."

The boys are Jenna's brothers. All three of them. I've seen them a few times, but they are working their butts off to buy a ranch of their own. They could take their parents' money and buy it today, but they want to earn it themselves and their parents are so proud of them for it.

"Thanks," I mumble and grab some coffee and a plate of food.

Eating is the last thing on my mind right now, but I know she won't let me leave the house without putting some food in me. She sits down at the table with me even though she only has a glass of water. This is one thing I love about being at Jenna's, even if you are the only one eating, they don't let you eat alone. After eating every meal alone growing up, it's a small comfort I don't take for granted. It's something I had at Mac's house too.

Nope not going there.

"Jenna said you had to head down to the police station today?"

"Yeah, they want to check my cell phone for any tracking stuff, and since I got the new one yesterday, I can just drop it off and get an update too."

"Is Jenna going with you?"

"You bet I am." Jenna comes bouncing in and sits across from me at the table, but her nose is right back in her phone.

"Jenna, put your phone down, don't be rude."

"Sorry, Mom, I just have some planning. I am looking at land in the area, the guys are going to be ready to buy soon and I think I want to help them out at least get started. I liked spending time on..." She trails off and gives me an 'I'm sorry' look.

"You liked spending time on the ranch. You can say it, it's okay. I liked being out there too, more than I thought I would."

I finish my coffee and food and stand up to put my plates away and Jenna jumps up.

"You ready?"

She has a bit more energy than normal and it makes me think she is up to something.

Like she can read my mind, she answers, "I promised Sky to let her know what happens at the station today and she is already asking."

I nod and we head out to her car. The police station is on the other side of town from where Jenna lives, and she is in the same neighborhood as Mac's family's lake house and Sky's parent's place. I watch the small town go by and catch glimpses of the lake and try not to think of Mac. But of course, any time I see the lake all I can think about is when we had sex there.

I should have gone to Dallas and stayed with Sky, but something about being close to the memories here just drew me in. It was like Jenna knew, she didn't even question it, just welcomed me in with open arms.

Before we know it, we are at the sheriff's office and as I walk up the stairs, I'm reminded of the last time I was here when I pressed charges against Lee. Mac and his dad were right beside me then.

I look over at Jenna and try to force a smile, but I'm sure she knows what I'm thinking because she wraps her arm around me and we walk the steps together.

Inside, we ask to speak to Ben and don't have to wait very long before he comes out to greet us.

"Sarah, I didn't expect you to be in town. Let's head back to my desk."

We sit down and he looks me over with his critical gaze that makes him a good cop. I feel like there is a neon arrow above me telling everyone we just broke up and to make sure I'm okay. Thankfully, I see Jenna shake her head slightly and Ben gets the hint and moves right on.

I pull my old cell phone from my purse and hand it to him.

"I got a new one, so I don't need that back," I tell him, and he slips it into an evidence bag and makes some notes on his computer.

"Do you want an update on the case?"

I take a deep breath and Jenna grabs my hand and doesn't let go.

"Yes."

"Okay, well Lee is still down in Rock Springs. He will face trial there before coming up here to face trial and I'm guessing, serving his time in Amarillo. That will give us time to put our case together. He sat down with a lawyer and they are trying to get him less time, so he gave a huge testimony against your parents. We did find tracking software on your laptop that matched his story and the bank documents that came in this morning show sums of money leaving Lee's account and those same sums showing up in your parents' accounts to the penny. Not very smart."

"That all happened in the last forty-eight hours?" Jenna asks with as much shock as I feel.

"He lawyered up the second he hit the jail cell, and he knew there was a video of everything he said at the ranch. I have been watching this case personally too and pushing things along as I could."

Jenna gives him the side eye. "Why?"

Ben smiles. "Well, I know Sarah, but more than that I love Mac's family. I was a skinny, nerdy kid growing up and didn't start to fill out until the end of my senior year. The summer before my senior year I was being picked on downtown. Blaze and Colt saw, and they stood up for me. They didn't know me but saved my butt and we hung out a lot after that when they were in town. That family was always nice and welcoming to me and this is my way of returning the favor. I know how

Mac feels about you, you are family to them, so this makes it a top priority to me."

"They still let you on the case?" I asked, a bit shocked.

"Sarah, this is a small town. We know everyone, but I did disclose to Robert that I am a bit closer to this case than most and he said he would watch it too."

Ben offers a friendly smile then looks back at his computer.

"So, checking the notes, it looks like a warrant was issued for your parents but no news of if they were picked up. So I would just stay alert and once they are brought in I will let you know."

I nod, letting it all soak in. I've been so consumed with everything going on with Mac that I haven't given a second thought to my parents and them being involved with Lee on this.

"Thanks, Ben." I force another smile and stand up.

Ben walks over and hugs me. "I know Mac might kick my ass for this but, Sarah, whatever is going on, that man loves you. It's a love I rarely see anymore, don't push him out. Know that I am here for you too. If you need anything, call. I make a good designated driver any time day or night."

Jenna laughs and we head out as I'm lost in thought.

"Want to go get something to eat?"

"No, can we head back to your place? I need to do some thinking."

When we get back to her place, I don't say a word and just walk around to the back of the house and out to her dock on the lake.

The lake is like an old friend that is there for you no matter what, never changing but always new. The breeze of the lake always seems to wash away my doubts and fear, and I'm hoping it will have the same effect now as I slowly make my way to the end of the dock and sit down.

I look over the lake toward where Mac's family's house is, and even though I can't see their place from here I still feel my heart clench telling me I'm sitting on the wrong dock.

I look back across the lake I can barely make out the homes on the shore on the other side they are just tiny dots of color all muted together with the trees and the shoreline as my thoughts start to race.

Did my parents really do this? Did they sell me for money? What type of human sees their kid and thinks, 'well, we are going to lose the house so let's just sell her, we don't need her.'?

I start to seethe. I never got along with my parents and I always felt like I was a mistake. They told me many times I wasn't planned, and they had no intention of having kids. It was never followed with a 'but we are glad we have you' or 'you were the best surprise'. They had nannies for me who made sure I was fed and did my homework. When I wanted to go to a friend's house, I didn't ask my parents, I asked my nanny. When I needed new clothes, it wasn't my mom who took me shopping, it was the nanny. They took me to school, taught me how to wear a bra, was there for my first period, and taught me to drive. They checked out all my dates and took photos before prom. All the things parents should do.

The worst part was that there was a new nanny every year, they never kept one around longer than a year. They said it was so I didn't get attached, but I'm willing to bet it was cheaper that way.

Even on their worst days I never thought they were capable of something like this. The more I think about it the more it all makes sense.

They encouraged me to come home and almost made it sound like this would be different. I bought into it because despite it all, I wanted that relationship. Then they forced me to the diner like it was this huge favor that they'd got me a job there. I know Beth would have hired me on the spot, we left on good terms when I went away to school.

I don't know what the terms of the agreement with Lee were but I'm willing to bet there were daily updates. It makes sense why he always knew things and my parents were always talking to him.

Was Lee paying my expenses too? There aren't a lot, mostly my phone and my car. When I came home from school, they gave me a credit card for things I needed. I thought they were being nice but now my stomach sinks. Who was paying for that? Was it Lee?

I didn't put much on it, mostly I bought some interview clothes, all of which were trashed during the break in at the lake house. It slowly all starts to add up.

It makes sense why he lost his lid when I went to stay at Mac's lake house, and he and my parents didn't know where I was. It makes sense why my mom didn't want me to move out and why she wanted me to drop the police charges.

How wrong is it, that after all this there is still a small part of my heart that hopes my parents weren't as heartless as they've acted? That they were actually upset that Lee put his hands on me like, that they didn't approve of it like they seemed to.

I'm pulled from my thoughts when Jenna sits down beside me and hands me a Margarita.

"Figured the thoughts on your mind might be eased with one of these."

I laugh and hug her. I relay my thoughts to her, and she reassures me that she didn't even see something like this coming, no one could have.

About the time we finish our drinks, my phone pings.

I look and gasp, seeing who it is.

Mac: I just heard there is a warrant out for your parents. Stay safe, Sunshine. I love you and will always be there, just say the word.

I lie back on the dock and take in the evening sky that is starting to streak with color and sigh. My brain says I made the right choice, my soul is saying I made the wrong one, my heart is trying to get me to run to him, but my body is numb. There is no telling who will win this race.

Chapter 27

Mac

I am lying in bed at the lake house. Even though Mom had my room cleaned and redone, I just couldn't stay there, so Mom and Dad told me to take their room. Being able to see the lake from the bed just floods me with all the memories.

I just sent a text off to Sarah. I need her to know that nothing has changed for me.

I hear movement in the kitchen and get up and head out there to see what is going on.

"Sorry, I didn't mean to wake you, but I'm starving."

"It's okay, Sky, I'm not exactly sleeping." I sit at the breakfast bar.

"This is a good plan, Mac. If she says no, I'll just throw her ass in the lake like I used to do when we were kids."

"The slight chance that she would want to say no is what scares me, but knowing I can't live my life without her is what is pushing me to do it."

Sky makes tacos and we sit and talk for a bit, going over the plan again. Jenna and Sky text and Sky lets me know Sarah is okay and that she went to bed early, but it seems that everything her parents did hit her today and she is emotionally drained.

It kills me that I can't be there for her to help her through this, but I need to take a deep breath and do this right. I can't mess this up.

Just before midnight, my phone rings.

"Hey, Mac, it's Seth."

Seth is the Rock Springs sheriff and has been keeping me up to date.

"Hey, everything okay?"

"I just got word that Sarah's parents were picked up and booked. They didn't think they had done anything wrong, so they were easy to track down and were arrested at their house. They were booked without a fight. I don't think they know Lee flipped on them yet."

I let out a sigh of relief. "Good, so what's next?"

"Well, your girl brought her phone in this morning. I was talking to the guy on the case up there. He got a rush on it and turns out there is even more spy software on there, so good call on making her get a new one. They are lawyering up and the next steps depend on theirs. I think they will want your statement and whoever was with you when you moved Sarah's stuff out. It's not child endangerment, because she is over eighteen, but it can build the case. Get some sleep, it will be a few days before we hear anything else."

"Thanks, Seth."

I look at Sky. "Sarah's parents are in custody and there was more spyware on her phone."

"We should have thought earlier to have her get a new one."

"I had the same thought, but who thinks parents would do something like that to their own kid?"

Sky nods and we head to bed.

· · · · ● · ● · · · ·

Today is the day I get my girl back. Time apart is killing me and I can't wait another day, I need her in my arms. I need to know she is safe, and that I've done everything I can. I didn't sleep well last night as I went over my plan and what I am going to say, over and over in my head.

I've been planning and setting everything up since this morning. Sky has been working from home since she moved to Dallas because the start-up company she is working at wants to save money. This means they haven't gotten an office space yet. This thankfully allowed her to be here and pull my whole plan together.

I've put her to work with a few things, but her big job is getting Sarah here. She is on her way to Jenna's house now. Her story is that she just drove in wanting to be there for Sarah. Jenna knows what is going on, and when Sky suggests they head to her parents for dinner, Jenna is going to jump on it. They are going to get her dressed and ready.

Once they get here, they will come to the lake house instead of to Sky's parents' place that is two houses down. From there, it is all on me to do the rest. They made that part perfectly clear.

I hear my phone ping just as I am finishing setting everything up.

Jenna: Heading your way now.

Nerves hit me and I have to take a deep breath then walk out to the side of the house just out of view of the driveway. A few minutes later I hear a car pull up and then I hear her voice. It soothes my soul and makes my heart soar because I know I've got this now.

"I don't want to be here, Sky."

"I know, but humor me, there's something I think you need to see."

"This better be good."

I hear them walking toward me and when Sarah rounds the corner, she takes my breath away. She doesn't see me at first, so I take her in. She is in a black dress and black sandals but it's the simplicity that is just breathtaking.

When she looks up and sees me, her eyes go wide and she stops in her tracks. I smile at her before she speaks.

"What are you doing here?"

"This is my house, Sunshine."

"You know what I mean, why are you in Walker Lake?"

"Because you are in Walker Lake."

She looks off to the side and I slowly walk up to her and gently take her hands in mine and bend my knees trying to catch her gaze.

"Sunshine." When her eyes meet mine, I smile. It warms my heart, like the feeling when sunshine hits your face. The warm feeling that crawls across your skin and embraces your whole body.

"Riley got her test results back and it wasn't the stress from everything that happened with Lee that caused this. In fact, that might have saved the baby's life."

"What?" Her voice shakes and I see the tears building in her eyes.

"How much did Riley tell you about her past?"

"That her ex was abusive and when she ran, she ended up in Rock Springs and met all of you."

I nod. "That's right. She was with that guy for four years and never once saw a doctor until she was with us. I don't know the details, that's between her and Blaze, but some of that abuse caused her uterus wall and cervix to thin, and as the baby got bigger it would have caused more problems. The stress of that event allowed the doctor to find it before the issue got too big. She has to stay at home with her feet up and Blaze is waiting on her every need."

At this point, tears are falling down her face, but I'm not done. "In fact, there is one big thing stressing Riley out that Blaze can't fix and it's driving him mad."

I pause and wait on her.

"What is it?" she whispers.

"You."

Her eyes meet mine again as shock crosses her face, so I continue before she can speak.

"You are family, and you being gone and thinking that you are responsible for this is driving her crazy. She blames Lee and her ex, Jed, not you. You are one of us now and will always be. It's why I'm here, Riley and Mom both told me not to come home without you and I'm pretty sure it's because they like you better than me."

I see a small smile cross her lips, but she still hasn't said anything. It's time to go for broke.

"Take a walk with me, Sunshine." I tug gently at her hand and she nods and falls in step beside me. I walk down to the lake and as we clear the tree line the dock is in view and I know she sees it when she gasps.

"Mac... what is all this?"

"Come with me and I'll show you."

I guide her toward the dock. As the sun starts to set, it makes all candles and lanterns lining the edges glow and flicker. The dock posts are covered in twinkly lights and on the end is the huge bean bag seat from the basement that she loves to cuddle with me on, but now it's covered with a few blankets.

I take her to the middle of the dock and stop. I take a deep breath and hope she can't hear how fast my heart is racing.

When her eyes meet mine, I smile.

"This lake holds memories of the best part of my life." I look around and smile. I turn her to face the back of Sky's house and move to stand behind her with my hands on her hips. I turn her to face the shoreline.

"I saw you the first time, right there in that red bikini you wore all summer. You were just stepping out of the water and laughing with Sky. That's the day I walked over and said hello. Best decision I ever made."

I turn her just a bit, still facing the left side of the dock but looking at the shoreline in front of the lake house.

"This is where I spent so many hours those first years watching you, trying to hide how hard your sexy tan body made me. Memories that carried me between visits."

I turn her to face the other side of the dock.

"This is where I made you mine, Sunshine. It's where you tempted me with that barely-there thing you called a swimsuit and wrapped yourself around me."

I can see her nipples harden under her dress, and goosebumps coat her skin. I lean closer. "This is where I sank into you the first time. Where I took your virginity and gave you mine."

"Mac," she gasps, but I don't stop. I turn her around to face the beanbag chair.

"But this is my favorite memory." I see confusion cross her face, so I move to stand in front of her and take her hand. I reach into my pocket as my knee hits the ground.

"This is where I ask you to be my wife and spend the rest of your life with me because I can't live without you. Sunshine, the last few days have been miserable, and I don't ever want to go to sleep without you in my arms again. I need to take care of you and know you are okay. I have loved you from day one and I will love you until my last day. Be my wife, Sarah. Will you marry me?"

Tears pour down her face and it's ripping my heart out. She looks back over to the shoreline where we first met and then back at me.

"I dreamed about this day for years, Mac. I never thought we'd get here. Today is so much better than my imagination. Yes, I want nothing more than to be your wife." She throws herself into my arms and it takes a minute for me to register that she just said yes.

I hug her tight, then pull back and kiss her. "The last few nights I wondered if I'd ever get to kiss these lips again," I murmur against her mouth. I pull back and look into her eyes and wipe her tears away then reach for her hand and place the ring on.

"This ring was my grandmother's, and then my mother's. Now it's yours, I always knew it would be."

I kiss her again then take her over to the bean back chair.

"What's this for?"

"Here, lie down facing this way." I get her situated and then lie down next to her and cover us up with the blanket.

"This is for a great ending to my favorite memory here." I wrap my arms around her and pull her in, and a few minutes later there is a loud sizzle and a pop as fireworks light off overhead.

"You did this?" she asks in amazement.

I laugh. "I wish I could take credit, Sunshine, but no, this one was Jenna. She mentioned the fall festival the town was having always includes fireworks, so I looked up the schedule to make plans."

We sit on the dock watching the show as my heart finally settles for the first time in days.

Chapter 28

Sarah

I wake up and stretch and can't wipe the smile off my face. Last night was perfect. When we came in from the dock the girls had dinner ready for us, the four of us ate and talked and wedding planned all night.

When the girls left, it was just Mac and me, and we talked about why I left, and he settled my fears in a way I couldn't. Knowing his family sees me as family too puts a smile on my face. I always dreamed of being part of this family, it was the best part of every spring and fall getting to spend time with them.

"More sleep," Mac mumbles, and his arm around my waist tightens.

Today we head to Jenna's to get my stuff, then we head home. Mac pouted a bit when he realized we won't be able to drive together because I have my car.

I have to admit, I am excited to get back to the ranch. Walker Lake just isn't home anymore.

"It's morning, sleepy bones," I tease and run my hand through his hair.

His eyes slowly open and he pins me with his bedroom stare, and I laugh. "We don't have time for that, we have to get to Jenna's."

He grumbles, but we get out of bed and pack up the car, and head to see Jenna who is waiting on the front porch.

"Took you two long enough! Mom has been hounding me, she wanted to make you all lunch before you head down."

We spend the next hour packing up my stuff and eating lunch with Jenna and her family before we make the drive back to Rock Springs.

I pull into the ranch and Sage runs out and hugs me before I even make it out of the car.

"Don't you ever do that to us again. You are stuck with us. Now let me see the ring!"

"Oh my, we need to talk about wedding planning." Megan comes up to look at the ring too and I see Mac grinning from ear to ear behind them.

"I guess I should follow tradition and get married at the ranch church and have the reception at the event barn."

The girls cheer and start talking a mile a minute about dress shopping, decor items, and dates as we walk inside. The guys welcome me back, but a woman I don't recognize is sitting at the table as well.

She stands up and comes over to me.

"You must be Sarah, I'm Lilly, a friend of Riley."

"Friend of everyone," Blaze corrects.

I remember Riley mentioning Lilly, she's the truck driver who picked her up and brought her to Rock Springs.

"How long are you here for?" I ask her.

"Well, with Riley on bed rest, I talked to the office and switched my home base to Rock Springs for the time being, so I'm driving three days and home for four."

"She is staying here with us to help out and because Riley begged her to. So I put her up in a guest room and she has free rein of the place."

Lilly laughs. "These guys are amazing. I've heard all about you too, so I'm sure you know what it's like for them to sink their claws into you."

I laugh. "Yeah, looks like I'm stuck here now too."

I head upstairs and peek my head in on Riley.

"Girl, get your cute butt in here and talk to me, I'm so bored and you have the best story of all."

I lie down on the bed next to her and tell her everything; from my thinking and why I left, how I left, and every detail leading up to Mac proposing and every detail of the proposal.

"These Buchanan men are such romantics at popping the question." Riley sighs.

I sober up quickly. "I really am sorry for all the stress I put you under."

"Girl, I thought you said Mac told you! This wasn't your doing, the person to blame for this is Jed. That bastard, I can't say I'm sorry he's dead after everything he put me through. But what's going on with my uterus rests solely on his shoulders." She hugs me the best she can. "Now talk to me about everything wedding planning."

We spend a few hours talking before dinner and I feel so much better. A feeling of home and family fills me, and I can't seem to wipe the smile off my face.

That night after dinner, I ask Mac to take a walk with me out to the ranch church where we sit in the back corner and talk wedding plans and life in general. I wiggle onto his lap and rest my head on his shoulder.

"Remember when you asked me what I would do if I could do anything?"

"Of course I do. Do you know what you want to do, sunshine?"

I smile. "I do. I want to be right here and be a rancher's wife."

"Sunshine..."

"Mac, when you asked me that question, this is what popped into my head. To be here and be your wife. But it wasn't ever this simple. I didn't think this was possible for so long that I had to come up with a plan B, and that was to get away from my parents."

With his face buried in my neck, he just breathes me in before speaking.

"This is the life I always wanted too, Sunshine. I will fight day and night to keep it and I will chase you anywhere you go, so don't get any bright ideas of leaving me again."

"That was the stupidest thing I've ever done."

"I agree with that."

We walk back to the house after the sunset, under the big Texas moon, and I smile because I am finally home. All those years I pretended this family was mine, I now get to live my dream.

Epilogue

I don't remember the last time I have seen everyone in this house so happy. Mac hasn't stopped smiling since he brought Sarah home last week and even with everything going on with Riley, Blaze is still in good spirits.

I watch Colt help Sage with dinner, and he can't keep his hands off her. He keeps hinting at making babies of their own and she keeps saying to wait another year.

Ella keeps telling Jason the same thing, she wants to get through school before they have babies and he grumbles and agrees, but I can tell he's proud of her.

Megan and Hunter are in the living room arguing over what to watch. Her little baby bump popped today according to Hunter. She is around three months along, but because she couldn't button her pants today, and he insisted she stay home with her feet up.

I smile and shake my head as I take a snack upstairs for Riley.

"Oh, thank you! I don't know why I am craving ants on a log so much because I haven't had it since my parents were alive, but now it's all I want to eat."

I sit in the chair Blaze had brought in for those hanging out with Riley. It's crazy comfortable and even has heated and massage seats.

"Well that little one is going to rule your life for the next eighteen years as least, so you better get used to it," I joke.

"Thank you again for coming, Lilly, I'm so pleased you're here."

"I like it too. Wasn't ever a ranch person, but there is something about this town that calls to me. It's relaxing."

She nods lost in thought as she eats her snack.

"So, I've seen you texting someone, is there a certain boy who has caught your eye?"

I laugh. "No, it's just Mike asking about something for the tractor."

"Mike the ranch hand?"

"Yeah."

"And why is he asking you?"

"Because you can't run a big rig and not know how to fix one in a pinch. Plus, I grew up with my dad as a mechanic, so I learned."

"Well, I think I'm going to take a nap. Why don't you go see if you can help him out?"

"I'm sure he's got it taken care of."

She smiles. "Well okay, but I'm still going to nap."

Once I'm downstairs, Sarah greets me. She has been in full on wedding planning mode since they got back from the lake house and she has been all smiles about it.

"So, I have my wedding dress appointment next week, did Riley tell you?"

"No?"

"Well, she said you are to go in her place and have her on video call the whole time."

I laugh. "I wouldn't miss it."

Mac walks in with grease on his hands.

"Mike still struggling with that tractor?"

"Yeah, told me to get out of his space with a few choice cuss words, so I left him to it."

"I guess it's time for me to go help out then. Riley just fell asleep for a nap, if someone wants to check on her in a bit."

I head out to the barn, taking in the ranch. It's so peaceful here and full of life. I love coming here between runs. What Riley doesn't know, is that right before she landed in the hospital, I sold my house in Tulsa along with most of my furniture. I rented a small storage unit for the rest and picked up more stops to run as they came up.

I've been with the company now for going on six years, so I have my pick of routes and stops. I don't want to drive a semi forever, and it's time to step up my game and save money to build my dream. What that is I've still yet to discover.

So being able to stay here was perfect timing and it was really easy to scale back down to spend time with Riley. I don't mind living out of my truck, but life on the road is pretty damn lonely and it's hard as hell to meet someone.

Meeting someone wasn't on my radar much until I watched Blaze's brothers fall in love one by one, and what girl wouldn't want a sexy cowboy who looks at you like you hung the moon and the stars, treats you like gold, and loves you with everything he has?

"God damn piece of shit," I hear a gruff voice yell, and the sound of what I am guessing is a wrench hits the floor.

I walk into the barn and see Mike kicking the tractor tire.

"Well, I wouldn't work for you either if you treated me like that." I laugh which earns me a glare.

"Took you long enough to get out here."

"Well, I'm here for Riley and besides, it's been my experience that men don't like a woman coming in and showing them up."

"Guess it's a good thing I'm not that kind of man. I'm one who wants the damn tractor running and I don't care if it's you, me, or Kit Kat the damn horse who fixes it."

I laugh and roll up my sleeves and head over to take a look. A minute later I feel the heat of his body next to me.

"Well?" he asks.

"This is an easy fix."

A half-hour later the tractor is roaring to life and Mike comes over and sweeps me up into a big hug.

"That's my girl, I knew you could fix this, Lilly!"

I've never had a guy so excited that I fixed something that he couldn't in my life. I've also never had a guy set my skin on fire or make my heart race when he's around like he does.

I am in so much trouble.

• • • • • • • • • •

Want more Mac and Sarah? **Sign up for my newsletter and get a bonus epilogue! https://www.kacirose.com/Secret-Bonus**

If you want even more of your favorite Rock Springs couples make sure to check out the **Rock Springs Wedding Novella!**

Want Mike and Lilly's story? It continues in the Cowboys of Rock Springs, Texas in **The Cowboy and His Mistletoe Kiss**.

Want Sky and Jenna's stories? Find them in the Walker Lake Texas Series starting with Sky's in **The Cowboy and His Beauty**!

More Books by Kaci M. Rose

Rock Springs Texas Series
The Cowboy and His Runaway – Blaze and Riley
The Cowboy and His Best Friend – Sage and Colt
The Cowboy and His Obsession – Megan and Hunter
The Cowboy and His Sweetheart – Jason and Ella
The Cowboy and His Secret – Mac and Sarah
Rock Springs Weddings Novella
Rock Springs Box Set 1-5 + Bonus Content

Cowboys of Rock Springs
The Cowboy and His Mistletoe Kiss – Lilly and Mike
The Cowboy and His Valentine – Maggie and Nick

The Cowboy and His Vegas Wedding –
Royce and Anna
The Cowboy and His Angel – Abby and
Greg
The Cowboy and His Christmas Rockstar –
Savannah and Ford
The Cowboy and His Billionaire – Brice and
Kayla

Connect with Kaci M. Rose

Kaci M. Rose writes steamy small town cowboys. She also writes under Kaci Rose and there she writes wounded military heroes, giant mountain men, sexy rock stars, and even more there. Connect with her below!

Website
Facebook
Kaci Rose Reader's Facebook Group
Goodreads
Book Bub
Join Kaci M. Rose's VIP List (Newsletter)

About Kaci M Rose

Kaci M Rose writes cowboy, hot and steamy cowboys set in all town anywhere you can find a cowboy.

She enjoys horseback riding and attending a rodeo where is always looking for inspiration.

Kaci grew on a small farm/ranch in Florida where they raised cattle and an orange grove. She learned to ride a four-wheeler instead of a bike (and to this day still can't ride a bike) and was driving a tractor before she could drive a car.

Kaci prefers the country to the city to this day and is working to buy her own slice of land in the next year or two!
Kaci M Rose is the Cowboy Romance alter ego of Author Kaci Rose.

See all of Kaci Rose's Books here.

Please Leave a Review!

I love to hear from my readers! Please **head over to your favorite store and leave a review** of what you thought of this book!

Made in the USA
Columbia, SC
23 September 2024